COLLECTED SCIENCE FICTION SHORT STORIES: VOLUME SIX

A SHORT STORY COLLECTION

RAYMOND S FLEX

CONTENTS

The Fields of Immortality   1
Lifeless Beauty   27
Boundary Wires   37
Viewing Chamber   69
The Company   77
Cul-De-Sac   99
Nothing Painted White   117
Ruptured Sky   147
Scripting Madness   169
Habitat   195
Hope Is A Horizon   215

Author's Note   241

THE FIELDS OF IMMORTALITY

The pain was sudden and overwhelming.

A searing heat all over.

Ash felt his whole body tremble. When he reached about, he felt the ground.

Solid rock.

It was sure, secure. There was something reassuringly *natural* about it.

He had fallen onto a ledge. Two or three storeys above the river below, gushing through the gully in the fading afternoon light. He had landed on his shoulders. That had sent shudders up his spine and down the backs of his legs. The back of his head had struck the rock too. And although his climbing helmet had taken much of the impact, his brain still felt like it had been shaken about within his skull. As he had fallen, he had made desperate grabs for the rock face. That had damaged his hands. He thought of all the training he had done — and how he had violated each one of the rules on how to handle a fall like that.

Then again he had believed he faced certain death.

But he was still alive.

He had survived.

The heat was most intense at his left hand. He tilted his head to look. He had to squint slightly — it was getting dark fast — but he saw the bloody stump where his index finger had been. The upper segment was also missing from his middle finger.

His muscles seized up.

His breathing became shallow and rushed.

For several seconds, all he could hear was his own heartbeat. Thick, percussive. It seemed to batter him deeper into the ground.

And then he picked out the tinny, mosquitolike sound. He shifted his attention upwards.

The security drone. It had blasted his ropes as he had been climbing.

It was ascending. Giving him up for gone.

Dead.

The pain racking his body was so intense that he could think of nothing else. He had forgotten how he had got here. What he was *doing* here. And then he remembered her.

He glanced around. He was disoriented. Everything looked different from where he lay. His pain caused the world to swill and spin. He saw Cara on the other side of the gully.

Gripping tightly to the rock face.

Her climbing ropes still intact.

Frozen in fear.

A warm wind swept through the gully. She jerked her head around. Her wild eyes met his. Already he could see the drone making steady progress towards her. He knew it would've learned. He knew that it would try out the same trick.

Take out the safety ropes and watch the climber fall.

Ash tried to shift his weight to one side so he might prop himself into a sitting position. The gesture was so painful he nearly blacked out. He sank his teeth into his lower lip until he tasted blood. Somehow it seemed to soften the pain in the rest of his body. The pain he felt in his hand from his missing finger. He couldn't give up. He could still do something.

She was in danger.

With his good right hand, Ash took hold of the rock behind him. He dragged air into his lungs, feeling a tightness in his ribs. But he ignored the sensation. He closed his eyes and hauled himself up. He sat slumped against the rock, his legs lying before him. His toes inches away from the edge. Even through his extreme pain — delirium drawing down over him — he knew he had got lucky.

So lucky.

He peered upwards. To Cara.

The drone was almost level with her now.

Its quadcopter blades shrieking.

He willed her to go for her backpack. She had a laser blaster in there. But she wasn't responding. Panicking, he reached about. Grabbed hold of a piece of rock. He rammed his arm against the rock face, staggering to his feet, his whole body screaming for him to crumple back down.

But on trembling legs, he resisted.

His hand gripped the rock tightly. He whipped his arm back. Tossed it upwards with all the force he could muster.

The rock struck the other side of the gully.

But missed the drone by some distance.

Ash swore at himself. He looked around desperately at his feet for another rock. He saw several. But when he looked up again, he knew the chances of him hitting the drone — of distracting it in some way — were slim to none. He had to do something else.

Or he would watch Cara die.

His lips worked faster than his mind. He called out. "Leap at it! Kick it out the air!"

Cara remained fixated on the approaching drone, apparently unable to hear him below. He wondered if the rush of the river or the shriek of the drone washed out his words. He prepared to shout out again. But then he saw her crouch back, beckoning the drone closer.

Ash saw the drone's laser cannon charging.

Taking aim.

It would be all over in a matter of seconds.

Cara kicked off against the wall. She cried out as she leaped into thin air.

The drone attempted to bank.

But it was too late.

Cara caught its underbelly with her fist.

The drone staggered. One way then the other. Trying to regain its balance.

Cara dangled in mid-air, at the end of her climbing rope. It held strong. She peered down at him then back to the drone. It was struggling to keep itself level. Cara had damaged something. But it was still able to fly.

"Shit," Ash uttered under his breath, feeling for the rock face, trying to ease himself into a better position to see above. He padded the pockets of his ripped jacket, trying to find something. He had lost his backpack in the fall. It had tumbled into the water below. Within it had been his own blaster pistol. If he had thought about it — if he had thought they might come up against some resistance — he would've strapped it on for the climb.

Now, though, it was too late.

The drone fired.

The shot whistled past Cara's head and smashed a hole in the rock, sending fragments scattering. Cara cried out but held her nerve. She grabbed hold of her rope. Got up momentum and swung herself back against the rock face.

The drone swirled among the air currents coming up from the gully. It was now waggling from side to side — unable to get any stability. Ash knew that it wouldn't be long before whatever self-preservation protocol it ran commanded it to limp home for repairs.

The drone fired another time.

This time it hit Cara in the ankle.

A wild, lucky shot.

She let loose an animalistic bellow. But she had managed to grab onto the rock face. She had a good hold. And Ash could see she was above the drone as it struggled to ascend.

If only she could find a loose rock ... or something.

Before Ash could call out to her again, she doubled over, grabbed hold of her boot. The foot the drone hadn't hit with its laser blast. She worked the boot loose and then tossed it at the drone, striking two of its rotor blades.

Ash's jaw latched open as he watched it spiral to its death in the river below. The small splash and muted sound it made on impact with the water seemed almost anticlimactic.

Seconds ticked past. Ash slowed his breathing. He felt his heart pounding against his ribs. The constant beat of pain rushing around his body.

———

"Jesus Christ, look at your fingers," Cara said, now kneeling before him.

Ash opened his eyes. He had dropped back down into a sitting position as Cara had descended the rock face to where he had landed.

"We're supposed to find the finger ... and the other bit, and put it on ice."

Ash summoned a smirk and nodded to the river below. "Only we've got no ice and the bits of finger are down there somewhere. And it's getting dark. There's no medic that's gonna be able to fix that. Always did fancy having a super-strong cyborg finger."

"We've gotta get clear of this place. We're still in danger."

"Right. And how'd you reckon we'll do that?"

"I ... don't know."

Ash traced his mind back. This morning seemed such a long

time ago. He thought about how he had risen early. Whenever he had an operation the following day he never slept too deeply or long. He and Cara had been deployed about three klicks from this position. Their current position was supposed to be two klicks from where they were right now. Their extraction point — once they had gone through with the mission — would be another five klicks from where they were. He glanced at his watch. "Shit. The window for extraction is in five hours. We're wasting time. We've got to get on with the mission."

"It's over — we can't carry on like this."

"I can't carry on. How's your ankle?"

As if she had forgotten all about her own injury, Cara straightened up and then glanced down to the frazzled ankle part of her boot. They could both see the burn mark where the laser blast had hit. It was a mess of scorched leather and blood.

"You're lucky that thing didn't blow your foot clean off. Doesn't that sting just a little?"

"I shot myself with some painkillers before I climbed down. That reminds me ..." She slipped her backpack down her shoulder, allowing it to fall with a thud at her toes. She unzipped and rifled through it, her tongue pointing out of the corner of her mouth as it always did when she concentrated on something. She withdrew a spray from within. Gave it a shake. "Okay," she said. "Which part's hurting the most?"

Ash chewed his lower lip again. He felt pain jangle every nerve in his body. His mind was screaming out for relief. "Nah — save it for yourself. You've gotta give yourself a chance to complete the mission. Get clear."

Cara's voice wobbled as she spoke. Although Ash was constantly surprised by her resilience, he was also always taken off-guard by moments such as these when the whole rest of her appearance seemed just a wrapper for the little girl underneath. "But what about you?"

"I'll be just fine." He nodded to her boot. "Take that off. Let's see the damage."

Cara hesitated but then did as he asked. She sat down opposite him and carefully loosened the laces of her boot. She clenched her eyes closed as she wiggled the boot down off her ankle and past her toes. When she had got the boot off, she let out a sharp exhale. "Christ. That *burns*."

"Take more painkillers if it gets too much. But try not to take too many to make you woozy, okay?" He glanced at her feet — now both of them were bare as she had tossed the boot from her good foot at the drone when she had knocked it out of the air. He could see that she had cut her good foot on the climb down — the sock was damp with blood. "You're not gonna be climbing out of here without any boots."

"Then how're we gonna get out?"

"There's two ways ... all right, maybe three, but the third one's kinda permanent." He saw from Cara's pallid expression that she had picked up on his insinuation and he scolded himself for trying to be funny at a time like this. They needed to concentrate. This wasn't just about them and their survival. This was about what had to be done. "One. Climb out of this gully, like we planned to. The drone was a surprise but we know about it now. You strap on your blaster this time, okay?"

"How're you going to get out?"

"That's the second way out." Ash nodded to the river flushing through the gully below. "A watery exit. This river winds its way within a klick of the extraction point. All I've got to do is keep myself floating along then haul myself out at the right spot. I'll meet you there."

"But can you swim ... like this?"

"I don't know. But I'm gonna try. Because I sure as hell can't climb out of here." He nodded to her backpack. "Now, come on, we've gotta get a move on. Light's going. You need to get into position."

———

Gloom overwhelmed everything now.

Even though Ash had insisted he was fine, the only way Cara would eventually leave him was for her to administer him some painkillers. Ash had to admit that he was a touch ashamed at just how grateful his body felt for the relief. His heartrate slowed. His mind was calmer. And everything had a kind of warm, fuzzy look to it. He also knew he'd been stupid to try and refuse. It was a weakness of his that made him want to act the dumb noble hero all the time. Then again, he supposed that was the type of character which this line of work attracted. She hadn't complained too long about taking his boots. Although she had argued that they were too big for her, he had told her that there was no way for her to get out of the gully without something on her feet. And since Ash would soon have a soggy bottom — and a soggy everything else — there was no point in him ruining a perfectly good pair of boots. She had bound them as tight as she could manage around her feet.

He had watched Cara up the rock face until she disappeared from sight beyond a ledge. Initially she had wanted him to help himself down to the river while she watched ... as if she would be able to help any if something went wrong ... she would only be putting herself in further danger if she tried to help. Although Ash had thought nothing of dragging himself down the rocks unaided, Cara had insisted on checking there was enough rope. He was thankful for her pragmatism — even if it had been borne out of a sort of maternal concern — because he knew it would've been too much for his crippled body to attempt.

And he surely would've slipped and fallen.

Then died.

Ash put Cara out of mind. He knew that if she got herself up out of the gully, she would switch onto the job at hand. He had no doubts in his mind that she was capable of seeing through the mission without him. If she hadn't been capable, she wouldn't have been chosen.

He busied himself with the rope Cara had left him, securing the screw in the rock face, giving it some trial tugs, and then working himself downwards. She had wanted to give him her torch, too, but he had refused to take it. Once he got clear of the gully, he would measure his location using his watch. Like all of their navigational equipment, it used a low-energy cloaked system so there was almost no chance of him being tracked by the signal.

All the same he didn't have it switched on the whole time.

There was such a thing as not tempting fate.

Ash tried to use his favoured right arm to guide him down the rope, but his forearm trembled uncontrollably and he switched arms. It felt awkward to use his left arm but at least he could support his weight on it.

He fought the urge to speed up, taking care with exactly where he was placing his feet on the rock face. A couple of times he was certain he heard that nasal whine starting up again — a fleet of drones maybe on their way — but whenever he paused to listen closely, to block out the rushing water filling his ears, the sound faded. He concentrated on the task at hand.

It was only once he landed on his feet on the firm ground below that he realised just how unstable he was. That he could just about manage to stand when he leaned heavily against the rock face. He cursed himself for having got into this state ...

He could've strapped on the blaster.

And he would've told Cara to strap on her blaster too.

That would've avoided the whole thing.

A moonbeam shimmered in through the crack in the gully above and Ash made out the glassy surface of the river. The water rushed on past. Much faster than it had seemed from up above. And he could feel the chill coming off it too. A shudder passed across the surface of his skin. He clenched his teeth and closed his eyes.

Once he had taken a couple of steps, the current dragged at his calves. The water was freezing. It sent lightning bolts daggering through his nerves. There was little physical fight remaining in his damaged body. Trembling now, he staggered a few times, attempting to stay upright, before he sploshed into the water.

For several seconds he was completely submerged. His body ached with the chill, and the pain of his injuries, but he forced his arms to push down and he kicked his legs.

When he surfaced again, he dragged down all the air he could manage, inflating his lungs, keeping himself buoyant.

The current was carrying him away.

He maneuvered himself around so that he was on his back.

Floating on the surface.

Looking up at the night sky.

———

Ash's mind drifted off to another place several times. It was the strangest sensation. On one level, he was aware that he was still here — floating on down the river — and at others he was completely gone.

Drifting in outer space.

Spinning about in the middle of galaxies.

Soaring past stars.

He had been a space cadet back in the day, but his eyesight had never really been good enough, and then he had flunked basic scripting a couple of times and he had decided he was better off finding something else. But he still had the desire to get up there, among the stars.

Whether or not it would ever happen, he couldn't say. At his age, it was out of his hands. Or so he liked to reassure himself. Still, what he was doing now wasn't a million miles away. And who knew where it might lead?

Ash checked his watch half a dozen times. He had no way of communicating with Cara because any such system would attract too much attention. It would present too much of an opportunity for them to be tracked. He could only hope that she was on target. Although he hadn't said as much to her, he had certainly selfishly thought to himself at the time that his best chance of getting out of this alive was for Cara to reach the extraction point, update the team on his condition, and have them send out a search party.

Then again, that also relied on the assumption that they deemed him worth saving.

Or that they were worried about him cracking under interrogation.

His watch began to beep and he knew he was closing in on the point he had selected. He thought he could make out the form of pine trees in the gloom and knew that he had reached an ideal spot for his exit.

His whole body felt stiff as a plank of wood but he forced his legs to kick. Wrenched his arms up out of their sockets and dragged himself towards the inner curve of the river. He planted his feet, feeling the sharp pebbles between his toes. The force of the water felt as if it might snap his spine. But even as he felt the pressure, he resisted, wading his way out of the water, his sight constantly fixed on the trees as if the point represented some oasis.

Back on dry ground, he heard the water dripping off him onto the surrounding rocky slope. Shivering, he picked his way, wincing each time he dinged a particular frazzled nerve in his body. He could think of nothing but the painkillers Cara had stashed in her rucksack. He kept telling himself that once they had been extracted, there would be a nice, warm hospital bed awaiting him with all the sedatives he could wish for on tap.

He had almost made the pine trees when he sensed something was wrong. It was something in the air. In his mind he was a deer, being stalked by an unseen hunter.

Rifle cocked.

Ready to fire.

"Stay where you are! Raise your hands! Get them up — *higher!*"

Ash followed the direction of the voice. Several paces to one side of the trees. In the darkness. He saw nothing but an eerie projection — the moonlight spotlighting an empty stage. He knew they had a distinct advantage over him. They were wearing night-vision goggles.

"Drop your weapon!"

Ash found his voice. "No weapon — goddammit!"

There was a host of calling-outs among the unseen people and then the sound of rocks slipping under boots. It was coupled with that unmistakable zipping, swishing sound of combat fatigue polyester rubbing together. Someone grabbed him and twisted his wrists behind his back, securing them with cable ties. The same person gave him a shove, making him stumble forward, almost causing him to trip over his own feet.

"C'mon!"

Wanting to get a final look at the river, Ash glanced back over his shoulder. He got a slap to the side of his head for his trouble. His vision flashed red.

"Face forward!"

Feeling his nerves flaring with pain, he concentrated on putting one foot in front of the other. He hoped — more than anything — that Cara had got herself clear.

———

The man's voice was grainy but with a crisp punch to it. He knew this wasn't someone he should mess with. "Just what were you hoping to achieve here, exactly?"

Ash felt increasingly bleary. He was finding it more and more difficult to keep his thoughts focused on the present. His mind kept getting away from him ... obsessed by the pain which racked every inch of his body. A white strip light burned above his head. The sort of functional, even lighting that they liked to use in offices, schools ... prisons.

He examined the windowless cell he had been placed within. It was just about large enough for him to take a couple of strides in any direction. There was a stone bench on which he sat and a metal toilet with no seat or any other embellishments.

The voice was coming from a grating in the door. The opening was about the size of a letterbox. He could see no details outside other than the vague suggestion of movement. He knew that the light was turned off in the hall to keep the identity of the speaker anonymous.

Ash said nothing.

"What happened to your fingers?"

Ash resisted the urge to look at his hand.

"You are injured. If you answer our questions we will see what we can do about your recovery."

Even though part of him screamed for him to find some relief — however he might obtain it — another more pragmatic part thought only of the agreement he had signed up to by accepting this mission. It would mean going against his word to answer the question. And he had always been a stubborn bastard.

He remained silent.

"Your companion is dead. She was intercepted just inside the facility. She decided to fire her weapon. She thought she could take us all on. We knew there was someone else out there because she was wearing men's boots ..."

Ash crunched his teeth together. He felt his heartbeat pounding at his temples. He knew he couldn't trust a thing this man said. He might just be trying to draw a response out of him. And yet Ash couldn't help himself. "Drone footage didn't show the two of us?"

There was a pause on the other side of the door. "Very well done. I thought you might've forgotten about that by now."

"That thing damn near killed me."

"Your companion killed one of my men."

"Then you killed her."

"She was trespassing." A brief pause. "Where were you to be extracted?"

Ash said nothing. He cursed himself internally. He knew that the man had succeeded in getting him to talk. That was the first step. When you got someone to talk, it was only a short hop, skip and a jump to getting them to open up on just about anything.

"It's not going to be that easy, is it?" the man said. "Very well."

Ash thought he heard the snapping of fingers, but it might as easily have been some mechanism clicking into action. He focused on the door of his cell, watching as it slid back.

The darkness beyond was overwhelming.

The man stepped into the light. He wore baggy combat

fatigues, a sunhat pressed on over his greying hair. He was squat and slightly hunched. His skin was tanned and his features were crooked and crumbling from what looked like a lifetime spent outside. He was in his late-fifties, perhaps. He wore no medals or insignia.

"Follow me," he said.

———

Ash had once read that whenever a cat was injured it did its absolute best to hide its pain. Although it had been domesticated over centuries — *millennia?* — mollycoddled by humans, it still had this hangover from its feral roots. He felt just like a cat now. And he was all too aware that he was doing none-too-great of a job of hiding his own pain.

The man led Ash along a corridor. There was a pair of armed guards on his heels. A male and a female also dressed in fatigues. Each carried a blaster rifle.

The man opened up a door then showed Ash inside.

Through the window, for the brief second or so the lights were switched off, Ash could make out the plains sweeping out beyond in the moonlight. He could make out several pine trees — just like that copse he'd hoped to make on his way to the extraction point.

To his rendezvous with Cara.

Was she really dead?

Once the lights came on, his focus shifted to his immediate surroundings. There were pictures on the wall. Several photographic portraits of men in uniform, sitting in rows, all of them wearing the standard-issue grin. Behind the desk, there was a whiteboard with several technical sketches on it. With a glance to him, the man rounded the desk, picked up the eraser and swept it through the drawings. Replacing the eraser on a shelf below the whiteboard, he said, "I don't reckon this is what you're after but it never hurts to play it safe, does it?"

The female guard took up her place at the door while the man ushered Ash into the seat opposite the desk. A few moments later, the male guard entered the room, bearing a glass of water. He placed it on the desk in front of ash and then retreated to the door.

Ash had the urge to ask him for something stronger. Hadn't the man mentioned something about having someone see to his injuries? He was beginning to shudder. Even staying seated in the chair was a challenge.

"Name's Woodman. And you are?" the man asked.

Ash remained silent.

"There just the two of you on this operation?"

Ash said nothing.

The man — Woodman — tilted his head back, exposing his stubbly chin, a few globs of dried blood where he'd nicked himself last time he'd shaved. "This your first time here or you been here before?"

Again Ash didn't respond. Because of his aching body, it took all his effort to stay seated. He wanted to leap up.

"What'd you reckon we should do with you?"

Ash met Woodman's gaze for a fraction of a second and then turned his attention to the window. There was little point as all he saw was a reflection of himself and Woodman there.

"Turn you loose?" Woodman said. "A little catch and release?" He sighed. "Yeah, we used to do that in the old days, when people came looking. We figured that it might be interesting to tail intruders. See where they came from. Who their connections were. And then they increased in number and ... well ... it just became *unimportant* ... we found out enough." He smiled slightly. "What we're doing in this place just about everybody on planet Earth is after."

Ash stirred from his daze. From his aching body. From the

constant pain signals going off in various nooks and crannies. "And what's that?"

Ash expected a dry chuckle. Perhaps for Woodman to shake his head in disbelief. However, instead, Woodman bowed his head slightly and interlocked his fingers, as if in prayer. "Immortality."

———

Ash's heart tapped hard at his throat. He implored himself to steady his breathing. He needed to give the impression of being in control ... no, he needed to do more than that —- he needed *to be* in control.

He felt the fresh night-time air strike his cheeks. It sent a tingle up his spine. And through his many aches and pains. Blood continued to pound up to his brain, telling him with each one of his strides that he should stop. That he should keel over. That he was defeated.

But he forced himself onwards.

In the bright compound floodlights, he focused only on the backs of Woodman's ankles, telling himself he had to keep going. That as long as he was still moving forwards he was making progress. He was getting closer to that hospital bed and the beginning of his recovery.

"You wouldn't think much of it," Woodman said, over his shoulder. "I mean, if you just *stumbled* across this place, you would think it was some kind of low-priority military checkpoint. And, well, there is no strategic advantage to this place. Then again, I suppose that's the key to all top-secret facilities. Why would you put it any place someone might stumble across? It also gives you the definite advantage of knowing exactly what anyone who comes to visit is after."

Ash glanced to the two guards, still trailing them. The female guard stared at him long and hard, as if considering whether she should raise her weapon. If he was a threat. He wondered if they would shoot him right here and now if he put up a fight.

If he tried to flee.

He chanced a glance at his watch and saw that he was only an hour from extraction.

He imagined the stealth quadcopter doing a sweep of the area and — finding no one — returning to base.

The possibility of escape raised a wild hope within his chest. And yet — at the same time — he knew that it was a vain hope. That he was barely in a condition to breathe properly, let alone make a run for the extraction point.

They arrived at one of those warehouses which'd always put Ash in mind of a gigantic tin can that'd been sawn in half and laid on its side. It was about two or three storeys wide — a hundred metres long. Sizeable enough to conceal great secrets.

Woodman underwent a bioscan — scanning both retinas and both hands — and the doors buzzed open. It was only when Ash had taken several steps inside that he realised the guards weren't following. That they waited back at the building entrance.

He was alone with Woodman.

He couldn't help marvelling at Woodman's confidence. That he felt Ash was not a threat given the condition he was in. That seemed a stretch. But then again Ash didn't really know the sort of people he was dealing with. He had an inkling of how high up a compound such as this one stretched but he wasn't completely sure.

Within the building, stark strip-bulb lighting pressed down. Ash's eyes had to adjust all over again. A couple of scientists in white coats passed by but neither of them made eye contact. It was as if the two of them were a pair of ghosts.

Woodman leaned into him. "You're hundreds of times closer

than you would've got if you'd snuck in here. I imagine you'd like to get your hands on your camera and go snapping away." With a wry grin, Woodman mimed taking photographs, like some shutterbug tourist.

They reached the end of a corridor and took the turn to the left. Ash read the labels on the doors. Nothing more than alphanumeric codes. They didn't appear to be in any sort of sequence. Woodman's gaze seared through him. "Before we go in I want you to know that I lied to you."

" 'Lied to me' ?" Ash replied.

"You see, there's such a thing as misinformation when you are dealing with hostiles. It's important to create a sense of confusion."

Already, as Woodman engaged the door, as it swept back before them to reveal the room beyond, Ash knew what Woodman was talking about. "She's alive — Cara's still alive."

"Not exactly."

The room opened out before them. It wasn't much larger than a classroom capable of seating thirty or forty pupils ... though there were no whiteboards, no desks, and certainly no teachers. There were, however, a series of naked bodies lying on their backs, prostrate within transparent glass cases. Each body was submerged up to its earlobes with a silvery liquid.

Ash couldn't help but be put in mind of coffins. Their body positions brought to mind the Corpse Pose — or Savasana — from a few yoga classes he had attended.

Before long, he eyed Cara among them. Just like the others, she had been stripped naked, laid on her back in one of the transparent cases, the liquid coming up to her ears.

Ash glanced to Woodman, expecting him to be wearing some kind of maniacal grin, however he instead wore a stony expression, as if he was thinking deeply about the sight presented to them. Perhaps he was thinking deeply.

Ash approached the case containing Cara's body. Woodman remained at the door while he did so. As Ash stood over the case, he peered down at her face. She wore a slight smile, or maybe he was reading too much into a neutral expression. His heart raced when he allowed his eyes to sweep downwards — over her elegant neck and breasts — to the burned-in blast mark at her stomach. No one could've survived a shot like that.

Above his head, there was a whirring sound.

Ash twisted his neck to look, feeling his whole body rattle with tension and pain as he did so. A large metal disc hung from the roof above Cara's body. When he extended his range of vision to encompass the rest of the room, he saw that each body had the same device lurking above it. His breathing shallowed.

"You wanted to know what we do here." Woodman said, still standing at the door. "Well, this is the short and thick of it."

Ash had the overwhelming desire the smash the glass case in which Cara lay. To free her from that strange, silvery liquid. And from the menace of the circular *machine* which loomed above. It was still whirring, the disc turning in a slow circle. Now he sensed Woodman standing at his elbow. His voice dropped to a near whisper.

"Scan her entire bio-matter," Woodman said. "Get a shot of the whole thing." Ash glanced to Woodman who tapped his temple. "Work out how it's all connected to the old CPU. Connect the dots so it can rebuild on its own terms."

"But ... immortality ...you don't mean these people are all still alive ..."

"They'll never wake up, if that's what you mean. Think of it more as purgatory. These poor souls are stuck right in the middle."

"Vegetables?"

"If you prefer to be blunt about it. But there's more to it than that. Because of their participation in this project there's a much better chance of them being able to escape their near-death condition."

"How?"

"Well, admittedly, these bodies might well have run their course, but their memories, personalities, the way that their brains *work* shall be preserved, studied, broken down, and rebuilt. Who knows, generations from now — maybe sooner — these people will walk again in some manner or other. Immortality."

"And what did these people do to sign up to the project?"

This time Woodman smiled. "Why, you thinking of putting yourself forward?"

Ash said nothing.

"Oh, these people come from a variety of sources. We want healthy specimens, mostly. Especially those who prove themselves resilient."

"The types of people who would try to break into a top-secret compound in the middle of nowhere?"

"Precisely those kinds of people."

Ash stared at the side of Cara's face. He watched as the disc descended, pausing only inches away from her skin. It appeared to be scanning her body — starting at her head, moving to her chest, and then ending up all the way down at her toes. As the machine worked, he studied Cara's face, seeing how her expression twitched, similar to how she might appear while sleeping. Then again, from what Woodman had said, maybe it was a kind of sleep that these subjects were undergoing.

Ash glanced back over his shoulder, expecting to see the guards waiting there. But in truth, he knew there was no reason for them to be there. They would still be positioned at the warehouse entrance. This whole warehouse would no doubt be fully wired for surveillance.

Security would be aware of any and all goings-on.

"Is this where you tell me I can live or die?" Ash asked.

"Oh, I think as you've seen here, the question is not as clear cut as that."

"I can lie down in one of these cases or I can die?"

"Mm, closer to the truth, I suppose."

Ash felt a tightness in his chest. He thought of the extraction point. The quadcopter. He had gained the information they had sought. It had cost Cara her life but if he could return to them then it would've all been worth it ... but that was one gigantic *if* in his current condition. Then something occurred to him. "Did you offer Cara the same deal?"

Woodman looked him in the eye. "Of course. Everyone who participates must give their consent."

Ash looked about him. He felt as if the walls were closing in. He tried to fight the sensation. His ribs felt as if they were squeezing the air from his lungs. "I don't want to be a lab rat. Not one of my career goals."

"It's funny the road life takes us on."

"What if I escaped?"

Woodman gave a single, dry laugh. "Ha. You're not exactly in fine shape to be doing any sort of escaping, are you? What time are you being extracted? Wait, let me guess." Woodman closed one eye. "About now?"

Ash didn't respond.

"The offer is a good one. Think of it as you doing your bit for humanity. And, who knows, in the future you might wake up and everything will be different. You might have a chance to live again."

"Or I might die in five minutes in a fiery explosion when my people nuke this place."

Woodman pouted. "That's a possibility. But other than that eventuality, this is likely to be the closest you get to immortality."

Ash shifted his attention back to Cara's face. There was a quality he didn't like about it — the lifeless, waxy look to her skin. As if she had been embalmed. In a spate of paranoia, he wondered if this wasn't all just some elaborate setup. A stage which'd been cobbled together to confuse him. To *test* him in some way. But as the seconds ticked past and as his extraction window came and went he realised his predicament.

"This is the only shot I have," Ash said.

"It seems so," Woodman replied.

"Then I have no other choice."

LIFELESS BEAUTY

The heat on the underside of Danica's wrist was nearly unbearable. More than anything, she wanted to lurch forward and grab hold of the lumbering tattoo artist responsible for her pain. He was in his fifties, bald, gut spilling out over his too-tight leather trousers. His stink of body odour, his constant nostril clearing, the way droplets of sweat landed on her bare skin with a chilly tremor, made her want to rush for the door. To go suck some freezing January afternoon air from the smoggy, darkening street outside.

But she had committed to this.

And she was determined to go through with it.

Her first tattoo.

"Aincha gonna look?" the tattoo artist asked.

When Danica replied, she was surprised at how calm her voice sounded. She had never been all that good at going off at people. Maybe she needed to snap more often. "I don't do well with blood."

"It's all done — there ain't no blood."

Danica wasn't totally sure whether she could believe him. Granted, the pain in her wrist had dropped to a low-level throb, rather than the sensation of hot pins sticking her. But she was wary that these types of people were always game for a joke.

They probably *enjoyed* watching a client faint.

As reality returned — the fierce white lighting within the tattoo parlour, the ripe scent of disinfectant running through everything — she gently eased herself away from the squashy chair the tattoo artist had made her sit in throughout the procedure.

"Some of my best work if I say it myself."

"Really?" Danica replied, wanting to believe it.

She took a quick breath and then examined her wrist. Sure enough, as the tattoo artist had said, there was no blood. And there was the steady, pinkish outline, just as she had requested. And then the little strawberry. As she locked her eyes upon it, she watched as the ink beneath her skin moved slightly — how a glean passed over the strawberry, as if a ray of sun had emerged from behind a cloud. This was the whole thing that had pushed her over the edge into getting a tattoo. The fact that they could animate them now. She had seen the videos online — the ones with people who had had entire films tattooed onto their bodies. Others who had ditched their wristwatch for a tattooed clock face. It was all due to the special form of ink that tattoo artists used. It had been commonplace for less than a year now and she knew that the uses for the technology would only grow, becoming wilder and wilder until the creativity was fully exploited.

Her own tattoo was far better than she might've expected. She hadn't wanted to go ahead and do something dramatic. Not right away. Not with her first tattoo. Already, she was toying with the idea of having a whole animated forest scene down her arm, complete with animals, wind, rain, and sunshine. It would looked incredible.

"Subtle," the tattoo artist said. "Much nicer than some of the stuff I've had done."

Danica couldn't tear herself away from the tattoo on her wrist. About once every ten seconds, the same, gentle sheen passed over the strawberry.

"Monotone pink. It's gonna keep its colour, that's the good thing. People that come in expecting a Michelangelo on their back and that their skin'll just be like a canvas for the rest of their lives, they ain't gonna get what they want anyhow."

Finally, Danica looked up. "Thanks so much. It's perfect."

The tattoo artist trod about the parlour, clearing away his

needles. Busying himself shutting up shop. When he noticed her looking, he turned. "Would you mind me asking why you got this little strawberry?"

Danica felt her gut twist. Her heart bounced into her throat. She thought up a hundred ways to avoid the question in the space of three seconds. But the tattoo artist held up his hand. "Sorry — I shouldn't have asked that. No right to, really. Tell you what, just for asking, I'll show you one of mine. Give you the whole story. That okay?"

"All right."

The tattoo artist returned to the stool on which he had sat throughout the procedure. He gave her a slight smirk. "You don't mind seeing some old guy's belly, do you?"

Danica felt suddenly self-conscious of how she had stripped down to her vest. And how she had picked out one of her tighter pairs of jeans that morning. Was there something about her appearance which might've been construed by some men as her leading them on?

... Goddammit, why was she fooling herself?

Men were led on by anything and everything.

"No, it's okay," Danica replied, fidgeting with her ponytail, poking a few loose strands of her black hair back inside the band.

"Name's Dave, by the way. Think if you're gonna look at some old guy's tats then you might as well know his name, huh?" The tattoo artist — Dave — grunted and then unbuttoned his baggy chequered shirt. He allowed the shirt to drop to the ground and he turned on the stool so that she had an unobstructed view of his back.

Danica took in the portrait on Dave's back — seeing the picture of a nude woman among some trees. As with the strawberry, Dave had done on her wrist, the tattoo was animated. To begin with, Danica wondered if the tattoo Dave had had done on his back wasn't a million miles away from the one she had in mind for her arm at a later stage.

She sat and watched as the scene played out on his skin.

First of all, everything was static. Like her own tattoo, there was only one colour — in Dave's case that colour was black. The sky was overcast. The oak trees crowded in among themselves, darkening the form of the woman beneath them. The woman clutched her nakedness, her long, tangled hair covering her breasts and waist.

"This was what I wanted," Dave said. "At the beginning."

Danica breathed in, only half conscious of the disinfectant in the air, of Dave's lingering sweaty odour. She watched on.

Slowly, the woman tilted her head back, looking out from Dave's skin. Her eyes were wide, and they were black. Danica felt as if they were the kinds of eyes you could easily slip into and keep on falling without ever hitting the bottom. For several seconds, Danica was certain that the woman was looking at her, waiting for her to make some sort of move.

Then something startled the woman from within the forest.

She doubled over and in her crouched position hid behind one of the oak tree trunks. Overhead, Danica noted how the skies were darkening. The forest beyond was growing gloomy. Soon the whole picture had darkened, other than the woman huddled over in the foreground. She peered out for breathless moments, clearly praying silently for help.

Strangely, Danica felt a heat at the corners of her eyes. And before she could stop herself, she felt a pair of tears snake free and roll their way down her cheeks.

From the darkness, Danica made out a face in the gloom. A monstrous face. She took stock of the twisted, horned features. The wide eyes. Sharp, crooked teeth. And the claws sticking out from each hand. She felt her breath hitch in her throat. The monster was still in the distance. Perhaps ten, eleven trees from where the woman concealed herself. But the monster was headed in the right direction. There was nowhere for the woman to go ... she was pinned up against the edge of the scene.

Danica glanced up as if Dave might be watching this play out too, but, of course, he was facing the other direction. She supposed that he had watched countless times in the mirror. He would be replaying everything in his mind's eye.

As the monster snuck closer, Danica silently implored the woman to stay still — to not give away her position. But the woman rose a little way and peered around one of the trunks.

And the monster spotted her.

Danica gasped.

Dave's shoulders flinched, as if he too was living the scene taking place on his back.

The woman turned her back on the monster. She took a few steps, starting to flee.

But the monster was too fast.

It grabbed hold of her by the arm.

Spun her around — her hair artfully concealing her intimate parts.

For longer than Danica could manage, there was pure fear. Even as she thought it herself, she realised just how ridiculous she sounded. That she was *afraid* for this woman who was playing a part in some piece of animation on this man's skin. But, then again, was this any different from the countless films she had watched throughout her life? And how she had emotionally invested a little piece of herself in each and every one?

As the monster moved in to take a large bite out of the woman's neck, its claws easing their way up her side, taking its time as it prepared for a meal, there was a change in the sky above.

The clouds thinned out. A space appeared. A sunbeam pierced the clearing.

It set the woman and the monster in its spotlight.

Something changed in the way the monster held the woman. There was no longer the appetite to wantonly consume — to tear her limb from limb. Now the monster appeared to be caressing her. Holding her in his arms tenderly.

Danica drew breath. It was almost as if she could feel the monster's scaly skin up against her own. As if she could smell the sulphur on its breath.

Stare into the inkiness of its eyes.

With the introduction of sunlight, the forest seemed able to breathe again. The trees appeared the spread apart, to give the monster and the woman more room. Now it truly was like they were on a stage. The two of them began to waltz slowly.

This dance continued for about half a minute before the sky began to darken once more. Danica prepared herself, thinking that the monster and woman would revert to their former roles — namely with the monster cast in the role of predator and the woman in that of the prey. But they remained together. Almost clutching one another. It was then that the scenery behind them faded into the skin on Dave's back.

And the two figures were gone.

Danica could hear Dave give a sniff. Her gut twisted slightly. She felt as if she had overstepped the mark. As if she had trodden in a place too personal to pry.

"I'm sorry," was all she could muster.

"I'll be all right in a moment," Dave said, rising from the stool, going about pulling his shirt back down over his bare shoulders.

"I can tell you about my tattoo, if you like. About why?"

Dave tugged his shirt down over his front. He blinked several times, clearing the tears welling in his eyes. "I ... don't want to hear about it," he said. "Let me tell you something about tats. If you gotta explain them, piece by piece, then they ain't worth hearing about." He held out his finger to Danica. "So you don't go telling anybody about that strawberry, hear?"

Danica pursed her lips. She held her breath several seconds before responding. "When you asked about my tattoo ... were you ... testing me?"

"Listen, darling, all's I'll say is I'm glad you didn't come gushing out. That's a good sign. Sign that you did it for the right reasons, I reckon."

As Dave went about his tattoo parlour, packing the box of needles away, straightening everything out, Danica lost herself looking at her strawberry tattoo.

She wondered what story it told.

BOUNDARY WIRES

"Out past the boundary wires, out of town."

A male voice. Gruff, businesslike.

And then a swinging fist came into contact with the bridge of Benjamin's nose.

———

Benjamin opened his eyes. He was lying on his side. His head resting on cool, damp concrete. Oily puddles surrounded him. Some kind of alien landscape.

Was he even still on Earth?

The day seemed dimmer, as if a cloud had passed overhead.

He felt a dull pain at the side of his head from where he had struck the ground. He ran his hand through his long, greasy hair and felt a welt there. There was a much more intense pain coming from the middle of his face. When he brushed his fingers across his nose, the whole world trembled around him. A flash of pain seized his muscles tight and he gritted his teeth, battling the sensation. He tasted blood on his lips. Its rusty scent wafted up his nostrils.

His Link had also been knocked offline. He no longer had access to his retinal display, floating superimposed on everything. He no longer had his clock, or the familiar icons which represented his mailbox, among other items, and connected his brain to the city mainframe, HOST. Thinking about it, being offline was probably the most disorientating part of all.

When he tried to lever himself up using his elbow, a dizzy spell struck. The world spun in a wild blur. A high-pitched ringing filled his ears. His heart pounded, each beat echoing the blow which had brought him to the ground.

"Jesus, pal! He really got you!"

A gruff voice struggling to contain its excitement.

Through a bout of double vision, Benjamin blinked several times. His retinal display flickered into life for a moment, and then burned out once again. The grey concrete was an infinite expanse. He could easily lose himself in it.

"Here, take my hand."

Outstretched fingers appeared just before the tip of Benjamin's nose. There were thirty, forty of them. After a shake of his head, his vision came clearer, although things were still blurred about the edges. He reduced the fingers to five.

"Don't touch him, Eric, you shouldn't touch him. You're not supposed to move someone who's had a head injury. Concussion. We've got to call the Services."

"They'll be here soon enough. We're in-city, remember?"

The hand remained in front of Benjamin's eyes. A steady, reliable reference in an otherwise blurry, unstable world. Like a new born baby, or a kitten batting a ball of wool with its paw, Benjamin staggered for the hand. As he did so, he couldn't help noticing the tattoo on the back of the hand, between thumb and forefinger. It was a face. Some kind of monster's face. It wore a kind of grimacing smile. Not an unwelcoming smile.

The fingers wrapped about his palm. Strong, warm. A sure hold. Another hand supported his lower back, easing him up.

As Benjamin was whisked to his feet, he couldn't help wondering if the other voice hadn't had a point. A shakiness seized his whole body — turning his spinal column into nothing more substantial than a rotten stick of celery. But the hold was firm, and he knew he wouldn't fall. He had never been the most substantial of men. He didn't weigh much more than sixty kilos soaking wet. No fat, no muscle. He'd been described as runt-like on more than one occasion. He'd always let his hair grow longer to hide his scrawny neck.

Standing on his own two feet, knees still threatening to buckle, another pair of hands took hold of him by the elbow, stabilising him. He relaxed into them, trusting the strangers' grasp. Feeling an intense migraine beginning to stab his temples, he narrowed his gaze, trying to focus on his rescuers.

A man. A woman.

They were so close. Too close for strangers. And they were holding onto him so intently.

As if he mattered to them.

The man — Eric — was examining him in a stern manner while the woman wore a wide-eyed expression of motherly concern.

Benjamin brought Eric's face into full focus. He took in his wide, watery eyes and his balding pate. His remaining hair had the colour and consistency of straw. He had to be nearing his fifties, but he was broad-shouldered, well-built. Certainly strong enough to rip Benjamin in two if he had half a mind to. His tanned complexion made Benjamin feel anaemic by comparison. He wore a faded chequered shirt beneath a patched-up tweed jacket, a pair of beaten-up blue jeans.

The woman was about the same age. She wore her straggly, wheat-coloured hair in ringlets. Like Eric, her skin was weathered — she too had seen a lot of sun. She had on a similar get-up to Eric, although Benjamin couldn't help noticing that her clothes were well-ironed and in a generally better state. She wore bright red lipstick and a pearl necklace which jarred with the rest of her appearance.

Benjamin's staring prompted an introduction.

"By the way, I'm Eric, and this here's my second-cousin,

Tricky. We're in-city for the day. Just seeing the sights, you know, running some errands."

Such strange phrases. Who "saw the sights"? Who "ran errands"? You could do all of that through your Link, from anyplace you wished. What an inefficient use of time.

Benjamin tried to manually reconnect his Link to Host. His retinal display shimmered and then failed again. This disorientated him so he shut his Link off with a manual override. The thought of being disconnected made him feel even queasier.

"Jesus," Eric said. "You're bleeding pretty bad."

Benjamin breathed in deeply and then reached up and touched his nose. Sure enough, his fingers came away wet with blood. A shiver passed through his body. He had always found the sight of blood unsettling. There was something which reminded him — a little unnervingly — of mechanical grease. Humans were just biomechanical machines bouncing back and forth on the surface of the Earth, after all. Only sometimes one punched another in the face. Machines never did that. Not unless they were programmed to do so by a human.

"We saw it all happen," Eric said. "From across the street."

Eric was gesturing to the point where they had been standing but when Benjamin tried to look he was caught by a fresh dizzy spell. He breathed in deeply, trying to centre himself and then managed to find his voice, cool and distant. "... Yeah? You saw?"

This time Tricky spoke. "Out of nowhere, it was. He just swung at you. What happened? What did you say to him?"

"I ... I don't know. I don't remember ..."

"If you need witnesses we saw everything," she replied.

"Thanks, thank you ..." bile bit at the back of Benjamin's throat and he swallowed "... thanks for ... for stopping."

"Gratitude's got nothing to do with it," Eric said. "Just duty, isn't it? You wouldn't carry on by if you saw someone knocked over in clear daylight, now, would you?"

Even in his uneasy condition, Benjamin wasn't so sure. It was very easy to walk on. To pretend you hadn't seen. And what with all the automated surveillance in the city, there was really no reason for human witnesses — only in exceptional circumstances; electrical blackouts, or areas covered by faulty devices. The assault he had been victim of would have been duly recorded and filed for future reference by HOST.

They would find his assailant sooner or later.

As if in response to his thoughts, a police drone whined over their heads.

Benjamin tilted his head back and peered out of a single eye. He felt blood dripping from his chin. The dirty, near-black sky loomed above, threatening to crush them. It had grown darker still in the few minutes they had been standing here. There was a dampness in the air too — rain. He traced the drone's flight as it disappeared over the tops of the buildings.

"Hah!" Eric said. "Hah! See that, Tricky? They'll be following him now. Catch him up in no time."

"Good lord," the woman said. "Our good lord."

"Tricky's right, though," Eric continued. "You need to be seen to. You've got —"

A synthesised voice burbled into life. "Please step aside."

For a moment everyone froze. Benjamin's focus sharpened and his nausea slunk to the back of his consciousness. He eyed the dirty white humanoid form approaching from across the street.

A MedDroid.

Its stiff, articulated movements brought Benjamin into mind of a mechanical sloth. Its body was large, rectangular, top-heavy. It seemed improbable that the legs could support the bulk of its casing. But it staggered on.

"Please present left arm for examination," the MedDroid said, arriving before him, towering over the three of them at well over two metres in height.

Benjamin felt the strangers' grip on him slacken gently. It was a strange sensation. As if they were somehow taken aback, startled by this display. Had they never seen a droid before?

Feeling the throbbing pain in the centre of his face and the side of his head, he held the underside of his arm up for the MedDroid's inspection.

A bright red light — not unlike an old-time barcode scanner — passed across the veins of his left wrist. The sensation was warm and fuzzy. For a second he wondered if this was how a theoretical robotic foetus might feel within its mother's womb ...

The MedDroid held its head to one side, as if in deep consideration. In truth, Benjamin knew it was all just a collection of ones and zeroes. Artificial intelligence — not genuine intelligence. Routines communicating with sub-routines. Layer upon layer of simple instruction woven together. The appearance of complexity in technology was a misnomer. It was just a collection of simple building blocks. He supposed he had the gift of seeing things that way since he was a scripter. There was nothing to do away with the "magic and mystery" of tech like developing it as part of your day-to-day job.

When you were the one pulling the puppet's strings.

Right now, he imagined data packets sweeping through the air to the nearest router, feeding back information on his physical state to HOST. This, in turn, would be processed through whichever medical assessment sub-system was currently in use. Whichever version had been given the most up-to-date approval by the Medical Council.

"Pulse elevated," the MedDroid responded. "Stand by for full-body inspection." The MedDroid's red light swept his body.

"Head trauma detected. Concussion suspected. Link status, offline. Would you like me to attempt repair and reconnection?"

Benjamin hesitated a second, then realised the droid was addressing him. "Uh, sure, thanks."

The MedDroid's light changed from red to blue and Benjamin felt a ticklish sensation behind his eyeballs. Then, as if someone had flipped a switch to turn the lights back on, his retinal scanner flickered back to life — steady this time. He couldn't help but smile at this return to normality. And he couldn't help admitting to himself that — artificial intelligence or not — machines were able to troubleshoot code in a fraction of the time it would take a human scripter. Then again, Benjamin supposed that the original routines, the commencing algorithms, had all been written by scripters. The machines just joined the dots.

"Stand by for treatment."

Benjamin watched as the droid's arm closed in on him and sprayed his nose and the side of his face. He felt the bleeding cease and the throbbing in his head came to rest. He supposed the droid had given him a light anaesthetic too.

"Further treatment recommended," the MedDroid continued. "Subject conscious ... Level 5 Sub-Emergency Case. Transport to medbay?"

Benjamin looked about. He tried to remember what he had been doing — what had led him to this moment. But there were only those words, "Out past the boundary wires, out of town", that gruff, male voice, and then the pain in the middle of his face as the fist had struck his nose.

"We'll come with you," Eric said.

"You'd better get checked out," Tricky put in.

Benjamin glanced at their concerned faces, and then to the MedDroid, its head cocked to one side in imitation worry. He had worked on some aspects of the humanisation routines for droids and he wondered if some of his own code might even be behind this gesture. He glanced back over his shoulder, as if his assailant might've made a reappearance. He could no longer hear the whine of the pursuing drone.

Feeling he had regained his swagger with the return of his Link, Benjamin turned to the MedDroid. "Please detail recommended further treatment options."

"Observation and analysis."

Benjamin smirked. Then he looked to Eric and Tricky. "I think I'm going to go home and sleep it off." He tapped his temple, feeling a dull tremor of pain as he did so. "My Link is back online. If there's any change to my condition a droid will come running, take me to the nearest medbay. There's something about medbays which has never sat right with me — they always make me feel sicker than I am."

"Well," Eric replied, "where we come from, we always like to leave things to the experts. When we —"

"Really," Benjamin replied, cutting him off, "I greatly appreciate your concern but the "experts" can get all the info they want through my Link. They don't need me to go anywhere. If the patch job the droid did starts to weep I'll be sure to drop by a medbay and get it seen to, but I've got stuff to do" — a new message notification blinked across his retinal display — "deadlines to hit, you know?" He looked again at Eric and Tricky feeling a twang of regret at his abruptness. Coming across as rude or short-tempered had been an issue for him throughout his life. To tell the truth, he had never quite got the hang of people.

But they were all so slow-witted.

Nothing like machines which instantly grasped whatever you told them, provided you gave them the right information, did exactly what you wanted them to do. "Look," Benjamin continued, "thank you for stopping and checking on me. I would like to

46

exchange credentials just in case I do turn out to need human witnesses."

———

It was night by the time Benjamin made it back to his flat through the drooling rain. Although he hadn't wanted to admit it to himself at the time, there was something about Eric and Tricky which had given him the creeps. Perhaps it was like looking at another version of himself. Of what he might've been if he'd been born someplace else — just a few hundred miles away. He supposed he felt that way whenever he interacted with humans. As if they were a reminder of just how lucky he truly was. He thought about what would've happened if they hadn't come to his aid. The MedDroid would've shown up before too long. It would've helped him to his feet. Really, there had been no need for them to stop. It was voyeurism, really, pure and simple. That fascination so many of the underclasses had with spectacles ... with *shows*.

Benjamin liked to think that he didn't care too much about his appearance but he couldn't help catching a look at himself in his bathroom mirror. He was shocked at the purple and black bruising covering his nose and cheekbones — the bruise he had creeping out from beneath his hairline. The MedDroid had done a good job on patching up the wound. He could see where it had seared the skin back together. Once the swelling went down, he would be as good as new. Just as long as nothing came back on the report to suggest he had busted the cartilage in his nose with the impact from the fist or fractured his skull when he had toppled to the ground.

He changed out of his work tunic and khaki trousers. He saw that blood had got onto his clothes. He threw them into his washing machine on a high-temperature setting.

After he had taken a shower, he felt fresher, a tingling sensation still passing over his face and the side of his skull. He had regained his balance now. He felt more like his old self. When he put on his dress-down robes, he noticed there was a package waiting for him at the chute by his front door. He slid it open and withdrew the small package.

It was a bottle of pills — painkillers. As he held the bottle in his hand, his Link flashed up the prescription. He was to take three a day, with meals. And not to exceed the stated dose.

He set the bottle on the side of his kitchen counter and then went to lie down. He had been planning to do some work before turning in, but he had to admit that he felt a little woozy. He needed to get some rest.

———

Benjamin woke with a start. It was the middle of the night. Creeping into the early hours of the morning. His whole flat was pitch black. He felt wide awake.

He sat up in bed, absentmindedly rubbing at his nose, and getting a jangle of pain through his nerves for his trouble. He supposed he was probably ready for some more painkillers. As he shifted out from beneath his duvet, he realised there was an alert on his retinal scanner.

Somebody was at the door to his flat, wanting to be let in.

He thought for a moment, trying to square what was going on. He wondered if it was some kind of a glitch. If there had perhaps been damage to his Link when he had fallen.

That wasn't uncommon.

There were stories aplenty about people who sustained damage to their Link through some sort of blunt injury — or exposure to electromagnets — and continued on oblivious until some obvious bug presented itself. He supposed he was better-placed than most since he was a scripter. He knew — first-hand — which sorts of things he should be looking out for in a faulty Link.

And a phantom late-night caller would certainly qualify.

He would get it checked out tomorrow.

As he poured himself a glass of water from the kitchen tap, the alert appeared on his retinal display once more.

Somebody at the door.

He crossed the flat, glancing to the bottle of pills still standing on the kitchen counter, and then cracked open the door.

"Anyone there?" Benjamin asked in a low voice, not wanting his neighbours to think he had lost his nut just in case anyone was up late and listening.

A woman in her late thirties wearing a suit, with her blond hair swept back in a tight ponytail, stood on his doorstep. "Benjamin Ghass?"

"Yes."

"Justice Operative Nair. May I come in?"

"Uh, yeah ... Wait," Benjamin replied, beginning to turn side on to allow Nair past, before changing his mind and blocking the doorway. "What's this about?"

She nodded at his nose. "That."

Benjamin thought this through. His retinal display identified Nair as having legitimate credentials as a police official, registered to Port Archer Station. He stepped back from the doorway. "Please come in."

As Nair crossed the threshold, he watched her swift eyes sweeping all the details of his flat. He thought of how the justice operative's Link would be in constant communication with the police protocols and procedures controlled by HOST. The Link would be complementing Nair's natural ability, filling in the gaps, drawing her attention to whatever might present a clue.

"I have to say I'm a bit surprised," Benjamin said. "I didn't think a ... human official would be assigned to a case like this. I thought this would be routine, everyday. I ... don't want to be a drain on resources." He decided it was a combination of nerves and the aftershocks of the pain he was experiencing which was leading him to blather on. He decided to shut his mouth.

Her inspection apparently concluded, Nair turned her attention back to him. "Mr Ghass. Do you recall what happened yesterday?"

Benjamin breathed in deeply. "I ... someone punched me in the nose. I fell to the ground. Two people came to help. Then a MedDroid fixed me up. I came back to my flat."

"Before that? Before the assault?"

Benjamin stretched his mind. Why couldn't he remember what had happened before? Where had he been going? Where had he been coming from? He had been wearing his work clothes but that offered him no hint. He was often called out to different parts of the city for in-person meetings, that "personalised" touch which management seemed so keen on. They so wanted clients to see the human face behind the code.

"I don't remember."

Nair nodded as if they were playing a game of chess and Benjamin had made an ingenious, but expected, move. "What's the last thing you remember before the assault?"

"Nothing."

"I mean, the day before, earlier in the day."

Again, Benjamin thought hard. "There's nothing that stands out. It was a day just like any other. I woke up, had breakfast. You know how your body is on autopilot? I think I had a meeting in the morning ... and then ..."

Nair eyed him closely.

Benjamin shook his head. "Sorry."

Nair exhaled. "Okay — I'm going to share the footage from that day with you."

An alert appeared on Benjamin's retinal display. He opened it. Saw that there was a video for him to play back. He glanced to Nair, who nodded for him to proceed. Jesus, there was always something about cops which made him nervous, even though he was the most law-abiding, passive little cockroach there was.

The video began. It was in greyscale. Designed so that it would make picking out contrasting shapes easier. Benjamin used this type of footage as a variable in many of his scripts. He found that it allowed for better pattern recognition.

He recognised the scene straight away. It was the street on which he had been assaulted. Why he recognised it so quickly — when he struggled to recall so much as a second of what had happened earlier in that day — he was unsure.

There was nothing noteworthy about the street. Concrete buildings on either side of the road. A couple of large skips over-flowing with rubbish. The streets were slick and shiny with the drizzle which was falling. He waited. Then glanced past the superimposed image to Nair, who he realised was watching the video through her own retinal display at the same time. When he shifted his attention back to the video, a figure suddenly appeared on the pavement. Nair paused playback. It took him a matter of moments to realise who it was. It was himself.

He took stock of the tunic and khaki trousers — his workwear. And then the familiar skeletal frame. The greasy mop of hair. Seeing himself from the third-person it was hard to think that anyone would see him as anything else than some sort of a creep. He was leaning backwards slightly, about to fall.

"Did I just ...?"

"Appear out of thin air?" Nair finished. "Seems that way, doesn't it."

The video played on. He watched himself stagger backwards, tumble down onto the concrete. Struck by an invisible blow to the nose. He fell on his side, striking the side of his head. He felt a flash of pain in that spot right now and glanced over to the bottle of painkillers on the kitchen counter. He could do with a couple more of those right now.

The video came to a halt.

"I ... don't understand," Benjamin said.

"That makes two of us," Nair replied. She glanced about his kitchen then rubbed at her eyes which he saw were red with webbed veins. "You don't have some instant coffee or something, do you?"

————

With the acrid scent of coffee tearing through the stilted air of the flat, the two of them reviewed the footage multiple times, trying to come to terms with what they had witnessed.

After they had gone back through the video for what must've been the fifteenth or sixteenth time, Benjamin paused the frame. He thought he saw something. They had gone through the video, attempting to get to the exact moment when he appeared out of thin air — just like magic. There had to be something there.

There *must* be something there.

Because there was no such thing as magic.

"Look," Benjamin said, using the sharing tool on his retinal display to bring Nair's attention to a detail. "Right before I reappear there's a slight shift in the image. Like the video drops out. It's almost nothing. It can't be much more than a quarter of a second, if that. A pause short enough to go unnoticed. To be written off as standard latency."

"Okay," Nair replied. "You think someone stopped the footage and placed you there?"

Benjamin met her eye. "Can you think of a more likely explanation?"

"I'm happy to admit I'm all out of ideas." Nair gave a wide yawn then sipped her black coffee, wincing slightly at what must've been the bitterness. He had offered her milk but she had declined. She had told him that putting milk in coffee was like diluting gasoline with water. She settled the mug back on the table then glanced at him again. "You're the expert, you work with this stuff day in, day out, you tell me. Is it possible?"

"Certainly — only it would take something quite powerful. And precise. Some kind of localised EMP. Carefully controlled too. This had to be someone who knew what they were doing. The way that I appear in motion. It's as if ... as if I was somewhere else. As if the person who struck me was in another place. And I just, you know, *appeared* on this street corner."

"What about that couple?" Nair said. "You know, the man and wife who helped you up?"

"They weren't together. They were cousins, second cousins, I think."

"From out on the Fringes, according to their IDs. We all know what goes on out there." Nair smiled wryly. "I don't reckon I'm too wide of the mark."

Benjamin felt a sudden flash of anger. It was unusual for him to feel passionate about anything — let alone to act on that passion — but on this occasion he couldn't help himself. Perhaps it was because he was unused to human kindness being directed towards him. Like a flailing flame which needed to be protected at all costs. "They're just *different*, that's all."

Nair widened her eyes and shrugged her shoulders. "Whatever, I didn't mean nothing by it. All I'm saying is what everyone else is thinking. Listen, can you give me something to go on so I can get this case closed? That way I get to go home, and you get to go back to bed."

Benjamin decided to push things back her way. "Haven't you been able to catch the person who did it? The person who struck me?"

Nair shook her head. "You saw the footage. Nobody was there. Nobody hit you. At least not on that street corner."

"What about the drone I saw dispatched? Didn't that turn up anything?"

"It did a sweep of the whole zone. Nothing."

Benjamin had a sinking sensation in his gut. "Have you ever come across something like this before?"

"Oh, sure, every case is different. Nothing's normal on this job. We've got the procedures, the protocols, all the tech, but real life never quite seems to fit neatly into those kinds of things, does it?"

Benjamin thought of his own job. As a scripter, it was his job to anticipate problems before they happened and resolve them. But even though he ran everything through a plethora of check-sums and debug sessions there was always something which cropped up when he got to real-world testing.

"So," Benjamin continued, "if we go with the idea that someone stopped the footage. Placed me there. I ... I don't know ... it throws up more questions than answers."

"How so?"

"There are ways of doing something like this. In theory. But I have no idea why I would be tied up with something like this. It makes no sense."

"You say you can't remember anything else from that day. That's the key. You need to remember."

"Do you have any other footage? Any record of my where-abouts that day?"

"That's why I was sent here, in person. I need your consent. By law we're only allowed access to surveillance records with direct geographical connection to the crime taking place."

Benjamin thought about this for a beat. "Sure, go ahead. If it helps resolve things."

Nair gave a stern nod, as if he was responding in a way which she expected any halfway reasonable person to respond.

————

Once Benjamin had given his official permission — via his link — the footage arrived swiftly. He opened up the file which was a composite of his actions throughout the day of the assault. This time the footage was in full-colour. It was the raw feed they were seeing, the footage stitched together his movements throughout the day.

He watched on as he left his block of flats at seven thirty in the morning. That seemed standard. Nothing unusual. He also noted how he was wearing the same clothes he had worn during the attack. The same clothes which were now sitting in his washer, clean, awaiting extraction.

The footage followed him along the street, to the local MagRail station, descending into the underground tunnels which wormed beneath the city streets.

Benjamin couldn't help smirking slightly. "You couldn't do with another cup of coffee, could you? This could be a long day."

But it appeared as if Nair hadn't heard him. She remained engrossed in her own video feed. Benjamin returned his attention to the footage.

He watched as he jostled onto the MagRail, taking his place among the other passengers, all of them dressed in a similar fashion. Although Benjamin had never thought of himself as being fashion conscious, he supposed that some aspect of fashion had made an impression upon his unconscious mind since he was dressed just like everyone else. Perhaps he had always had some kind of will to fit in with his surroundings — and making himself look as much like everyone else around him as possible was the simplest way to achieve that effect.

In the course of the past month, he had been doing some work in the banking district. Helping to tighten up local security. Putting new scripts in place to guard against unauthorised internal transactions. As always, whenever he worked on code left behind by other scripters, he ended up uncovering problems upon problems which widened the scope of the work he had to do. It was an ability his employer was only too happy to indulge since it meant move billable hours for the client. And when would a client ever ask for a blatant security issue to go unsolved? It would only lead to greater losses later on.

When the MagRail stopped at Philiturn Station — the heart of the banking district — he expected to see himself get off. And while a large amount of passengers did alight, he remained on the carriage, taking a seat which had been freed up.

The video went on.

"I'm going to speed things up," Nair said.

"Okay."

Benjamin watched as the MagRail journey continued. He saw the carriage wriggle along the line. He thought of the overground locations of the stations the train passed by. Past the outer area of the banking district and out into the suburbs.

"Where're you going?" Nair asked.

"I don't remember."

There was silence again as they watched the MagRail continue its course. Leaving the city steadily further and further behind.

"We're coming up to the boundary wires," Nair said.

"Okay," Benjamin replied, as if he understood the full implications of this.

To tell the truth, he had always been somewhat fearful about the boundary wires. As a scripter they did not sit easily with him. It was where the reach of HOST began to dwindle. The infrastructure on which the Link was built became much patchier.

Nair sped the video on. The MagRail reached the terminus. South Exit. Benjamin watched on unbelieving as he made his way through the other travellers and out of the terminal building. As he had expected on passing over the boundary wires, the camera outside was a longer lens and the image was grainier. But he was still centre stage. The program picking him out in the security footage was still hard at work.

Automatic transports — AutoTrans — hummed past the South Terminal. He watched as he hailed one of these and got inside.

"You still don't remember?" Nair asked.

"No — not a single detail."

For a few seconds, the footage switched to an in-car view. It was unsettling to see his own face up so close. Benjamin tried to read something in his own face. To see something in the expression. To try and second guess his thoughts. But he had no recollection.

The video feed flipped to the driver's view, and the AutoTrans turned off onto the motorway. Benjamin guessed that he rode the AutoTrans for the best part of an hour — Nair sped up the video again. Several times, the image flickered into darkness. On a couple of occasions, there were entire minutes when there was nothing for them to view.

The image returned as the AutoTrans pulled off the motorway.

Benjamin pressed his fingers into his temples, as if he might stimulate his mind into recalling something. Into bringing back some detail. But there was nothing. He might as well have been observing a stranger.

The AutoTrans took a winding route. It passed through deep forest, past a great lake, and a series of fields dotted with sheep. A final long-range camera shot showed the AutoTrans sweeping in through a driveway, and onto a dirt track. Automatic gates closed behind.

The camera remained focused on the gates.

After a couple of seconds, Benjamin glanced up at Nair. "Has playback frozen?"

"No," Nair replied. "It's still real-time. But there's no coverage. Private residence."

Benjamin analysed the image before him. The wrought-iron gates. He had got a sense of scale of the entrance when the Auto-Trans had passed through. The gates had towered above the vehicle. They had to be three, four metres tall. Trees within the estate obscured any chance of seeing what was beyond.

"What do we do now?" Benjamin asked.

Nair didn't respond. She only sped up the video again. Skipping through the frames. Trees jostled slightly in the unseen breeze. A couple of AutoTrans passed the gate, but no one else passed through the entrance. And neither did the AutoTrans return.

Nair stopped playback suddenly. "That's it," she said.

Benjamin was confused for a second, staring at the frozen image. He was ashamed to say that he made nothing out. He didn't like things going over his head but he supposed this time he was going to have to swallow his pride. "I'm sorry, I don't see."

"The timestamp. It's the time of the attack. You're back in the city."

Benjamin glanced to the corner of the image, and realised that

Nair was right. When he spoke the next words, he instantly felt his gut turn at the stupidity of them. "But I didn't see myself leaving."

"No," Nair replied. "I didn't either."

Benjamin was determined to redeem himself. "We need to go there — to investigate."

Nair eyed him closely. "You're happy to do so?"

"If that will help clear this whole thing up."

————

It was eerie going over the same ground he had seen himself pass over in the surveillance footage. The two of them took the MagRail, got out at the South Terminal, and then hailed an Auto-Trans. Although Nair could have requested a pool vehicle, she had decided it would be best if they could trail Benjamin's footsteps as closely as possible. They might pick up vital clues.

Although Benjamin had to admit he was a little lost when they passed the boundary wires of the city, Nair seemed to know exactly where she was going. She didn't need her Link. He could tell she was actually physically remembering which way they should go from the footage she had watched.

Benjamin wondered how good his own memory was. He tested it so little. Whenever he needed to go anywhere in the city, he would enter the place he wished to go into his Link and he would be directed there. No brain power required.

Was that why he was in this predicament now?

If only he could have remembered ...

By the time they reached the wrought-iron gates sitting at the end of the dirt track it was midmorning. Neither of them had had so much as a wink of sleep since they had left Benjamin's flat. The gates were even more imposing in real life, especially after the two of them had passed through a dark forest and open fields to get here. It seemed as if they were in the middle of nowhere. They hadn't seen another soul since they had left the motorway.

If there was one thing which Benjamin had learned in all his years as a scripter, it was that there was always a reason for secrecy.

The gate had a secure-access system. A facial-recognition scanner. Benjamin could tell that it was scanning them in the AutoTrans — its invisible eye casting them in its glare.

The gates didn't open.

Even though Link coverage was patchy out past the boundary wires, the signal was strong here. A notification appeared on his retinal display — the same notification he supposed appeared on Nair's simultaneously:

Identify or leave.

The Link gave him the option to send his identification or close the message.

"You okay?" Nair asked.

Benjamin breathed in deeply. He had an ominous sensation about this whole thing. A sharp pain ran through his nose as if in warning. But what was he supposed to do? Should they turn around and go back to the city? Say nothing more about this? Close the case?

But now Benjamin had come this far, he knew there was no turning back.

With a nod, he sent his personal credentials and he guessed Nair had done the same, because after a short period the gates folded in on themselves. The AutoTrans crept through the gap, purring them cautiously along the uneven track.

A forest sprouted up around them, darkening the day. There were drainage ditches on either side of the track. Although Benjamin understood the practical requirement, he couldn't help but be brought into mind of the moats which surrounded medieval castles.

After ten, fifteen minutes, the trees thinned out and an expansive country estate opened out before them. Benjamin took stock of the mansion house — fifteen, sixteen bedrooms? — and the elegant driveway which curled around a marble fountain. As they got closer, he realised that the fountain was in the form of a gargoyle, spitting water from its throat. Although he was a long way from being superstitious, there was something deeply unsettling about the statue. He realised that Nair, too, was looking at this.

This was familiar.

He couldn't quite put his finger on it, but it was definitely familiar.

The AutoTrans came to a halt outside the front steps of the house. Benjamin stepped out of the vehicle, feeling as if he was being watched.

Knowing he was being watched.

It was then that he saw them.

The man and woman from back in the city.

Tricky and Eric.

Standing in the doorway.

Only this time they looked different.

There was no trace of the clothing they had worn the day before. Eric wore a white shirt over a pair of formal trousers, while Tricky had on a rosy pink dress. She was going barefoot and why not given the pleasantly warm day?

Benjamin's focus fell to the tattoo of the gargoyle on the back of Eric's hand. He thought about the fountain behind him. His only connection between the two moments in time — back on the street, and now ... was there another, deeper in the past?

Eric spoke. "So this is where the trail of breadcrumbs led?"

Nair looked uncomfortable for the moment. But she soon broke out of her daze. "Justice Operative Nair," she said, climbing the front steps, apparently so she wouldn't have the pair standing over her — dominating her.

Benjamin remained where he was. He wanted to size this whole thing up. He didn't want to get too close just yet. He realised that Nair had not put two and two together. That she didn't realise that this was the couple who had seen to him following the attack. For the first time, a little voice spoke within him, urging him not to say anything.

Not yet.

"I'm investigating an assault which took place yesterday," Nair continued. "In the city. We have reason to believe that some sort of incident occurred at this address. Would you grant us permission to have a look around?"

"Don't you need official endorsement for that, Officer?"

"*Operative*," Nair corrected them.

There was something off about their voices too, Benjamin noted. He couldn't help but feel that what he had seen the day before had been an act. This, now, was the real thing.

Or it was closer to the real thing.

"Of course," Nair replied. "If you'd like to have two dozen oafs forking through your carefully sculpted topiary ..." She jerked a thumb to indicate the trimmed hedges running up either side of the front steps.

"No," Eric replied, with a slight smile. "I suppose not. Please, come in."

There was still not the slightest trace of recollection of what had happened here — of having met Eric and Tricky prior to the attack. Benjamin felt uneasy. He wondered if he should run. He looked back at the AutoTrans. They had ordered it to remain where it was — to wait for them. And it would do so.

Apparently sensing this unease, Eric looked down at Benjamin as Nair slipped past him into the front hall of the house. "Aren't you coming in too? We've got apple juice. Freshly squeezed from the orchard."

Benjamin stretched his mind another few seconds.

And then something told him he was safe.

That this would be okay.

———

Benjamin stood at Nair's shoulder, deeply aware of how her eyes picked and turned over every last detail of the house. He could tell that she was a natural for police work. That this was something which had been hardwired into her DNA. It was the sort of effect that he strived to achieve when he wrote his scripts.

There was nothing that he put down as being suspicious, but then again he was a scripter not a justice operative. He was still reeling from the different characters of Eric and Tricky — entirely alternative to those he had "met" in the city following his assault.

"Shall we go through to the conservatory?" Tricky asked. "I can just tell that the sun is about to break out from behind the clouds."

"An excellent idea," Eric replied. "I'll go fetch some things from the kitchen — put the kettle on."

Tricky smiled at Benjamin and Nair. "This way, please."

They had only taken about half a dozen steps when Nair spoke up. "If you wouldn't mind, I'd like to take a look around the place first. Before we take afternoon tea."

Tricky paused. Her brow wrinkled for a second. "Certainly." She took up an easier expression. "That's what you're here for, after all."

Benjamin exchanged glances with Nair.

"What would you like to see first?"

"I just want to look around," Nair replied.

Although Benjamin had never been anything like a stickler for high-class manners, he had to admit that even he was a little taken aback by Nair's attitude. But, then again, he supposed this was the type of personality which made a successful justice operative.

"Might I suggest the attic?" Tricky said. "You get some excellent views out over the lake."

"Fine," Nair replied.

They climbed three flights of stairs to reach the attic.

As Benjamin took the final few steps, he sensed danger. Something was wrong. But before he had the chance to warn Nair, it was too late.

Nair crossed the threshold, into the attic. As Tricky had alluded to, there were large windows on all sides, looking out over the lake. The light was strangely dimmed in a way which told him that this was tinted glass — that it would be impossible to look into this room from the outside.

In the middle of the room was what looked like a dentist's chair. It had one of those circular light fittings hanging above it — one of those which was so common in dental surgeries. On the other side of the room, there was a set of shelves, freezer compartments on each. There was also a set of localised computer servers sitting underneath. Benjamin recognised this set-up right away. Private servers. Strictly controlled. These ones were almost certainly illegal.

The door slammed shut behind them.

Benjamin turned to see Eric there. He wore a solemn expression.

"What the hell — ?"

Before she could get out her words, Eric stuck Nair with a

hypodermic needle. Her eyes widened and then she passed out, falling like a ragdoll in Eric's arms. "Give me a hand, will you?"

To begin with, Benjamin thought Eric was speaking to him. But Tricky slipped past him and helped Eric set Nair in the dentist's chair.

Eric padded Nair down, finding a blaster pistol tucked into a holster beneath her jacket. He removed it, handed it to Tricky and then straightened up, wiping away the perspiration which had gathered on his brow.

"Okay," Eric said to Tricky, almost as if he had forgotten Benjamin was there at all. "Secure her — get the system online. We haven't got long."

Benjamin's whole body had seized up. He felt conflicting emotions. There was an overwhelming urge to step in, to help, to act the hero. But then there was something else, too.

Something more complicated.

"Once you're done with her, give him the same treatment as last time. That's what the contract says."

Benjamin finally broke out of his daze. "What contract?" he said, murmuring. It might as well have been to himself as neither Eric or Tricky replied to him directly.

He watched on as Tricky strapped Nair's arms and legs to the chair. How she worked with the efficiency of a well-trained technician.

Eric was working on something within his Link, interfacing with the local servers. What Benjamin had previously believed to be a circular light fitting descended from the ceiling and came to rest over Nair's collapsed head, concealing her face.

Tricky was finished. She turned away from Nair, approaching Benjamin. "Let's go," she said, the politeness from their arrival a memory now. As they made their way back through the house, Tricky spoke to him in a matter-of-fact manner. "In about five minutes' time you won't recall any of this. You won't remember us. All that will remain is a partially written-up police report into a commonplace assault." They reached the front hall and Tricky produced a syringe from somewhere. "Show me your arm."

Eyeing the needle, Benjamin said. "What about the justice operative? Won't they come looking for her? Won't they ask *me* questions? Won't they see the footage of us coming here?"

Tricky sighed. "Really, I don't need to answer. You won't remember any of this."

Benjamin felt a flush of anger. A sense of betrayal. He wondered if he felt so outraged because those kind people who had helped him up after the assault had never existed at all.

It had just been an act.

"If it's all the same, please tell me," Benjamin said.

Tricky glanced out of the window, to the driveway and the AutoTrans waiting outside. "We're not going to kill her, if that's what you think. We're not even going to keep her prisoner — not long enough to arouse suspicion in any case. We're not those standard psychopaths out in the countryside, waiting for meat to trip into their traps."

"Then what are you?"

"Scientists. What did you think?"

"I don't know what to think. I don't remember anything."

From upstairs, there was a high-pitched whirring sound. Benjamin recognised it as the kind of hum that an electromagnet, or some other charged device made. It was beginning to give him a headache.

Tricky met his gaze and glanced up at the attic. "You really need to learn your place. A contractor, that's all you are. You had skills which were useful to us, you have served us with those skills, and now you are no longer useful. We will supply your employer with excellent feedback, though." She gestured with her own arm. "Roll back your sleeve, please."

"Tell me what I've done here."

Tricky rolled her eyes. "We took you on about a week ago. You came out here. Set up our systems. Helped us with some scripts — for which we are very grateful. As part of what we are working on here — that part you do not need to know — we required a justice operative's mind. You came up with an ingenious plan of staging a crime in the city. One which would be impossible to solve. One which would confound the automated systems and assure a visit from a human operative. That part went very well, didn't it?"

"I don't know, I don't remember."

"Although I don't recall the exact details of your plan, the effect was to have it appear as if a ghost had knocked you to the ground. And to have the two of us standing around. Not so that we would appear to be suspects, but to arouse just enough suspicion that we would be treated as witnesses. For what it's worth, you asked for your mind to be wiped prior to the attack, although the contract states that the only mandatory wipe was to be on completion of the job."

"Why would I say that?"

Tricky shrugged. "Only you know the answer. Maybe you just didn't want to know?"

"I heard a voice — just before I was struck."

Tricky flicked the tip of the syringe. "Hmm?"

" 'Out past the boundary wires, out of town.' "

For the first time since they had arrived, Tricky smiled. It was as if none of this had happened. As if Tricky was the same character which remained in Benjamin's memory. "That was Eric's idea. He wanted to leave a clue. Make things *extra* obvious."

The hum above them was getting louder.

The smile slipped from Tricky's lips. "Eric will need me in a few minutes. We need to get going."

Benjamin stared at the needle. He tried to recall the contract he had signed. Ever having come to this house before in his life. But he remembered nothing.

And soon he would remember nothing of this, either.

———

The sun blazed in through the window of the AutoTrans. Benjamin watched the scenery going by. His mind idled along. His thoughts were muddled, a congealed mass which was impossible to make sense of. He supposed he had been out here — out of the city — on some sort of a job. That happened every so often.

"Out past the boundary wires, out of town."

There was something familiar about that phrase. Strange that those words should come to him right now. Was it something his boss said to him in a kind of mocking tone? Mocking him that he would need to leave the tender caress of HOST behind — that he would need to leave the comfort and stability of his Link behind?

He supposed it didn't really matter.

They were only words.

And the only use for words was to write scripts.

VIEWING CHAMBER

F lickering lights seared the backs of Uma's eyelids.

　　　Flashes of red veins.

Uma tried to get up. But her body was pinned down at the elbows and knees.

Pain rippled through her chest. Her heart stuck in her throat.

She was completely immobilised.

She attempted to remember. She tried to think through how she had got into this situation. But nothing occurred to her.

"Uma? Uma? Are you awake?"

The voice was soft, warm, and she recognised it instantly as her mother.

Only her mother had been dead for fifteen years.

"Mum?"

"You've been sleeping in late again, Uma. You can't go on sleeping forever. Not if you want to amount to something."

Uma felt as if someone had dragged a knife blade across her wrists. The voice — and what it was telling her — was so close to reality that the only conclusion she could come up with was that it *did* belong to her mother.

And yet she knew it was impossible.

"Uma? Wake up!"

———

Water hit her face like a concrete wall.

Uma gasped.

Her whole body jerked up.

She was free.

Lying on her back, on firm ground ... despite the water.

When she opened her eyes the whole world was blurred.

Impossible to make out.

She flipped onto all fours, then to her knees, finally staggering to her feet.

Group laughter pealed around her.

At first she thought it was directed at her.

As if she was some piece of performance art.

Uma breathed deeply, trying to get hold of herself. Her vision was starting to clear. The aspects of her surroundings were becoming sharper. Everything around her was black.

She reached up to touch her face, expecting to find it sopping wet, but it was dry.

She reached out and felt the soft material.

Curtains.

Black curtains.

Was she ... backstage?

"Charlotte?"

Uma jolted around. Even though she knew it wasn't her name. The voice was too close for comfort. She eyed a woman of about sixty, wearing a tightly cropped robe. Even in the darkness, she could distinguish her long white hair which reached down to her waist.

"Two minutes," she said, and then slipped away.

Uma wanted to ask "two minutes until what?" but something deep within told her that there was no need for the question. In fact, that asking the question would be some sort of a mistake. When she reached down to feel what she wore, she felt smooth satin.

A dress.

She never wore dresses.

Beyond the curtain, she heard someone speaking from the

stage. Their voice rebounding around the auditorium through a crackling speaker system.

A woman.

Her voice was throaty, uneven.

As if she was making an effort to sound more manly.

Uma snatched another breath. She padded the dress she wore. That was when she realised the laser blaster strapped onto the inside of her thigh. She slipped it free from the holster. Checked.

Fully operational.

Ready to kill.

Now she knew what to do.

What she had been put here to do.

Her mind prickled, and something within her came alive.

She felt more conscious of her surroundings than she had ever been.

As if she was some sort of wild animal.

She stalked her way along, blaster pointed at the ground.

When she saw the light, she knew she was close. That she was close to completing her purpose. She had only to take a few more steps.

She channelled into the words again.

" ... and humankind shall forever look upon our example and reflect on the glory of our achievements. Just as they did with the Egyptians. We are writing a new legacy. Something for the ages."

The crowd whooped and cheered this.

Uma slipped to the side of the stage, catching sight of her own face in a mirror. Instantly, she knew it wasn't her face. Although she was having trouble remembering exactly what her own face really looked like ...

She examined the person standing in the centre of the stage. A woman in her fifties, wearing bulky, baggy robes. Her figure was squat and her face pudgy. And Uma couldn't help but feel that there was something unpleasant about her expression.

Someone tugged at her arm.

Uma glanced around.

It was the woman from before. "Not yet, Charlotte. Not quite yet."

But then she saw the gun.

Her mouth gaped wide and Uma knew she needed to act fast.

She shot her in the temple.

A searing blast of light.

The woman crumpled to her feet without a sound.

Uma had no time.

She eyed the stage again.

That was her target.

It was instinct.

Pure and simple.

But the woman had been right.

She had to wait for her cue.

The woman was wrapping up her speech.

"Every morning when you wake up for another day of work, remind yourself of the legacy we shall leave behind. Let that be your motivation to improve the colony and so improve everyone's lives. This day better than the previous one." Grinning, the woman glanced to the side of the stage — straight at Uma.

Uma knew this was prearranged.

That she was supposed to step onto the stage now.

She thought there might be some last-minute nerves. A sense of thousands of eyes upon her. But her steps were steady and she was careful to hold her gun concealed from the audience. The woman only noticed the blaster when she was three, four paces away.

And by then it was too late.

It was as Uma always remembered.

Surprise.

Confusion.

Fear.

... And then death.

Uma counted the heartbeats after she had dealt the killing blow.

... Three, four, five ... six ...

A laser blast struck her shoulder, spinning her body around.

She dropped to her knees.

Another hit her back.

And then the unseen shooter finally found their target.

———

Uma pulled her face away from the mask. Her surroundings were cool, sedate. She took a sharp breath, as if waking from a dream.

She was sitting in a small room on a hard wooden chair. There were a few cardboard boxes around her, and a table on which she had set her apparatus.

The viewing chamber.

Although her immediate surroundings were calm, she could feel that the unmistakable sense of panic wasn't far away. People calling out. Feet stamping. Alarms going off.

Uma packed the viewing chamber away swiftly. It folded down into a thin case which — in turn — she stashed in a squashy sports bag. Once she lost herself amongst the crowd there would be nothing remarkable about her.

Especially amongst the panic.

They hadn't seen her face, and that would set them back hours — perhaps days — in their investigations. The authorities would need to perform an autopsy. Establish that there had been unauthorised access to Charlotte's Link. And then there would be the hump to get over. The realisation that someone had taken control of her body ... made her do what she did.

Only then would they search for an assassin.

And by then it would be too late.

She would be halfway across the universe.

Uma stepped out into the corridor. She glanced one way, and then the other, seeing the coast was clear. She merged into the crowd fleeing from the hall. From the deaths they had witnessed. Little did they know the body count was actually three, including the woman who had lost her life backstage.

It was so easy to be moved along by the crowd, as if she was a log being carried downstream on the surface of a raging river current.

As she felt the cool night air kiss the surface of her skin, she thought about those strange amnesiac moments when she had first woken in Charlotte's body. On reflection, it was always the same. How her mother always spoke to her — waking her, imploring her not to "waste" the day ahead. She decided this had to be some kind of bug in the code, or just the way that the viewing chamber had wired itself into her subconscious.

Each time it gave her pause for thought.

There had to be some price for cutting into someone else's mind and body.

And leading them to death.

THE COMPANY

D ozens of pairs of ears surrounded Lorne.

She felt them listening to her — and her alone.

Just willing her to make a mistake.

To say the wrong thing.

To say *something*.

The transport hummed over the landscape, levitating several centimetres above the ground. The steady, reliable vibrations calmed Lorne, setting her in a trancelike state. She peered out through her porthole, across the surface of the asteroid they had been dropped on. The asteroid they had been assigned to mine. It was just like all of the others, really.

Grey, ashen, covered with craters,

Lorne squeezed the grip of her auto-drill tightly. Her auto-drill was a bright-orange colour, about the size and bulk of her torso when it was packed away into its transportable form — as it was now. When operational, it would unfold so it stretched out taller than her height. She cradled the auto-drill close to her chest as if hers was special — as if it wasn't like the one which every single other miner within the transport had been issued by the Company. It was strange that the drill felt so precious to her. Maybe she clung to the drill so tightly just to have something to hold close.

So she wouldn't feel so alone.

There had to be two dozen miners crammed into the transport. Everyone was silent, their heads bowed. Lorne noticed how everybody else cradled their auto-drill in the same way, like mother apes shielding their offspring from the fierce jungle outside.

They were a long way from any jungle up here.

A long way from Earth.

Not that Lorne had any reason to feel sorry for anybody — and least of all herself. They had all made the choice to take on this work, principally for the money involved. There weren't many legal ways in the universe to make a tidy pile of cash so quickly.

"You think this looks a good proposition?"

Lorne continued to stare out through the porthole. A couple of beats too late she realised that the words were directed at her. She turned in her seat, looking at the man sitting beside her ... could he be called a "man" ? He had a blond fuzz across his chin and acne scars. He couldn't be much older than eighteen, nineteen. At a stretch, he might be old enough to be her son.

"You can never tell till you get out there," Lorne replied.

Her own voice sounded strangely alien.

It seemed an age since she had spoken with someone.

People in the Company didn't tend to chat much. It was as if a sense of mutual suspicion weighed down everyone. As if every-body was equally wary of revealing personal secrets to strangers. Whereas she believed that other precarious situations led to people opening up to others around them, she decided that the Company was different.

"This is my first time in case you can't tell. I'd just like to get out and get started, you know?" he said, looking beyond her, and out of the porthole. "It's the anticipation that gets me."

"Hmm."

There was a pause. And then. "What's your figure?"

"Excuse me?"

"How much are you looking to put together before busting out?"

Lorne felt herself flush. She was deeply aware that everyone in the transport was overhearing their conversation. Although the rumble of the transport did a good job of stopping voices carrying too far, she knew those immediately surrounding would be hanging on every word. It was difficult to do anything else when two people were chatting in an otherwise silent public space. Almost like standing in the middle of a stage before an empty arena.

"I'm looking at seventy, eighty kay. I think that'll see me comfortable. Be able to buy myself a lot out on the Frontiers. Nothing fancy but it'll get me set up, I reckon. How about you?"

Although Lorne had no intention of answering his question, she couldn't help but think of the earnings she had accumulated so far. To be honest, she had lost track ever since she had got past half a million. She might even be into seven figures by now.

She looked him in the eye. "More than I have."

The man considered this, clearly picking up on the signal that she wasn't in the mood for small talk. They drifted into silence again for five minutes. And then the man spoke up. "Where you headed once you've made your sum?"

"I don't have anywhere specific in mind."

"Somewhere nice, warm?"

"Yeah."

"That sounds good." He flashed a smile. "It's okay, I'll shut up now."

Lorne felt a slight burn through her chest. Even though she was wary of sharing with strangers — especially fellow miners — her parents had brought her up to have manners. She could still hear their chiding voices whenever she failed to measure up to their expectations.

It was something she needed to avoid, however.

So she suppressed those chiding voices.

————

The two of them reached their destination in silence.

Protocol was just like it always was.

The transport rising to a high-pitched, deafening whine, and then descending with a sigh, falling into near silence. It was always so quiet in the moments after the transport had come to a halt. It seemed such a natural point for conversations to start — and yet they never did. The young man sitting beside her had caught onto how things were. That making conversation was against the unwritten rules.

Through her earpiece — through her Link — a robotic voice instructed them to proceed to the lower deck. There was a strange sense of solidarity that Lorne always felt when she stood with the others — all of them in their dusty-grey overalls, all of them plodding their way towards the stairs leading downwards. She supposed this was what it felt like to be in the Services. To be part of a single organism. A single stated goal.

Then again, she supposed there wasn't all that much difference between the Services and the Company. Both used individuals working together to achieve their aims. But whereas the Services were well-organised, everything kept in strict order, to strict timings, the Company felt altogether more ragtag. Perhaps it was because anybody could come on board. And everybody was out for themselves. There was no denying that.

Lorne supposed it was more difficult to herd mercenaries than noble soldiers.

As she shuffled along with the other miners, clutching her auto-drill to her chest. She surprised herself by speaking up. "You never thought of the Services?" she asked the man.

He stared back at her. "No — never. Why, do you think I look the type?"

Again, there was that slightly uncomfortable sense that Lorne had overstepped a boundary. That she had come close to offending someone. But he was smiling. And she realised he was being playful.

"It's a solid option," she replied. "Good career progression."

"Yeah — if you want to get sucked out into space. Or if you wanna get yourself blasted by some half-cut punk."

"Things are hardly safer in the Company."

He shrugged. "I'm free here. If I want, this is the last day's work I do. Not the same in the Services."

"You've got an answer for everything."

"Suppose it's good to give answers, sometimes."

They shuffled down the steps, part of the larger group of miners. Although Lorne hardly ever looked at the people around her, she couldn't help but notice the dour expressions spread across their faces. Was it really this bad? Had things really become this foreboding?

What the man said was true ... there were no long-term contracts with the Company. You only took on the work you wanted. And then you left.

Or you didn't.

Exposure suits lined the walls of the lower deck. They had all been freshly decontaminated. There was something about putting on the suits which Lorne found vaguely joyful. It reminded her of when she had been a child and she would come home to freshly laundered bedsheets. She filed along with the queue, taking the next available suit. She set her auto-drill on the ground and pulled the suit on over her overalls.

Laying his own drill at his feet while he stepped into his suit, the man said, "You would've thought that we could leave our drills down here with the suits too, huh?"

Lorne glanced about, still all too aware that they were drawing attention to themselves by making conversation. Now that she had broken the taboo, though, she felt that it was easier for her to speak. "Nobody likes to leave their drill alone. That's your respon-sibility. Just about the only thing you *are* responsible for. More than that, it's what you make your earnings with. Anything happens to the drill during the shift and you're done. It's all for nothing."

"My name's Orlick."

Lorne held herself still for as long as she dared. She waited until the last possible moment. Until the very last second. "Lorne," she replied.

———

The two of them dressed in their suits and joined the procession of other miners.

When they reached the airlock, they were told to secure their helmets. The life preservation systems engaged. As always, Lorne felt a sensation as if she had just been sealed in a ziplock bag. As if someone had sucked all the air out of her.

And then she breathed steadily — taking in the dull, dank tasting oxygen from her suit.

She looked out through the tinted glass of her helmet, seeing the young man — Orlick — thinking that he didn't look anywhere near as nervous as she herself had been on her first shift with the Company. Then again, she supposed that young men usually had a ruthless, carefree streak. They believed themselves to be invincible.

That would change when he saw his first fatality.

Outside, the surface of the asteroid was illuminated by bright floodlights. Even with the tinted glass between her eyes and the light, Lorne felt the strength of it sear her eyeballs. She held up her arm to shield her retinas. When her pupils had adapted, she brought her arm back down, peering out from between the slits of her eyelids.

All the pits the Company dug were pretty much alike. It didn't matter where in the universe they did it. There was always the same white tarp covering the hole. And the same MedDroids queued up in an eerie diagonal line outside the entrance. The way that they were positioned to view the miners ambling into the entrance always put Lorne in mind of those stories back on Earth where silent, noble indigenous people would watch on as European explorers stumbled blindly into some exotic horror in search of fame and fortune.

Weren't they in search of fame and fortune here?

She supposed nothing had changed about human nature, despite all the lightyears they had put between themselves and Earth.

Within the pit, they stepped onto a lift which wobbled each time another miner stepped upon it. Lorne wasn't quite sure why, but she made a point of staying close to Orlick. She wondered if it was some sort of misplaced maternal instinct. As if she would be capable of protecting him from harm. If she had trained to be a medic then there was no way she would be here. There were far more comfortable ways to make a living in the universe than this.

Why didn't she try one of them?

It wasn't too late ...

The lift whirred down into the mine shaft.

A pair of lamps prevented them from being plunged into total darkness. Lorne tilted her head back to observe the shrinking circle of light above collapsing in on itself. Becoming a mere pinprick by the time the lift came to a shuddering halt.

Although she knew it was impossible, she caught a whiff of sulphur in her nostrils. Even though everything was silent within her suit, she sensed the unease of the miners surrounding her. She knew that if they didn't have their suits to hide inside, there would've been a whole host of nervous gestures:

Darting glances.

Scratching.

Mumbles.

She wasn't sure whether the absence of these gestures and sounds made her feel more or less comfortable.

The silence was soon broken.

Her earpiece crackled into life.

It was the foreman — based above them, orbiting the asteroid in the shuttle which had carried them out here from the Company mothership.

"Conditions generally good. Ambient temperature minus seventy-two centigrade. No hostile environmental variables. Estimated three-hour window for operations. Please leave the access lift and proceed to entrance chamber."

Lorne caught a look off Orlick. For the first time, he betrayed a sense of nerves. He held her gaze for no more than a second before turning away.

This was always the hardest part.

Leaving the lift behind.

The direct connection with the world above.

History was littered with stories of asteroid miners who became stranded below ground:

Machinery failure.

Cave-ins.

Even sabotage.

Once they had all left the lift, it rose back up the shaft behind them. She noticed Orlick glance back over his shoulder. There was no trying to hide his fear now. It was obvious. And understandable. How was he supposed to know that the lift was only returning to the surface so that it might load up their SalDroids — salvage droids which would collect the salvage and return it to the surface of the asteroid — and not leaving them here forever?

As the last of the exterior light vanished, Lorne's night vision mode flickered into life.

Everything came to her in a gritty light-blue.

The cave appeared much larger than before. The ceiling towering above their heads. She supposed it had to be about the same height as a cathedral. As she cast her gaze downwards, though, she soon realised it narrowed sharply into a tunnel through which only two miners could comfortably pass side-by-side at the same time. This tunnel had been dug out by Company droids, although it had been with SalDroids in mind not the miners themselves.

A timer appeared on Lorne's retinal display. It showed three hours and began to count down. The three-hour window the foreman had calculated. All manner of variables would have been taken into account. Possible collisions of the asteroid with other objects flying through space. Ultraviolet interference. Solar flares ... that sort of thing.

They had three hours to see what they could find.

Lorne drew deep on her oxygen. An amber light glowed on her retinal display, warning her that she was using her oxygen at an "unsustainable level". She wasn't exactly sure what that vague warning meant. How long would she have left if she continued in that way? Two hours? An hour? Half an hour ... less? She knew that the only result of her attempting to push the limits of this would be an enforced early extraction. The foreman could demand the extraction of any miner at any time if he believed it a threat to the safety of the shift — a threat to the safety of the miner themselves.

So Lorne eased off.

Like a serpent which had recently grown legs and dragged itself from the primordial swamp, the miners followed the tunnel ahead. As alcoves opened up on either side — sub-tunnel systems — miners peeled off and made their way.

Lorne's Link — through her retinal display — recommended routes for her to follow. She knew that other miners were receiving the same recommendations. Again, this was all judged by the foreman and his systems back up in the shuttle orbiting the asteroid.

It was only when Lorne looked around that she realised the only person with her any longer was Orlick. Now his eyes were wide. Clearly he had been spooked by something.

He requested to open comms with her.

She accepted.

"Are you okay?" he asked.

"Fine. You?"

"It's just ... we're all alone out here ... the last miner must've peeled off ten minutes ago. How much longer are we going to go on?"

"You mean how much further am *I* going?"

As soon as she had said it, she scolded herself for sounding so heartless. That was the problem, once you had spent so long on your own you learned to be bitter, defensive in your interactions with others. She supposed it was some natural sense of self-preservation.

"I'm heading down here," Orlick said, indicating the tunnel to their left. "It'd be nice to stick close. To have someone show me the ropes — help out if something goes wrong."

Now this was something Lorne had almost never come across.

A man asking for help.

And she supposed that was the main reason why she felt drawn to do as Orlick said.

Out of curiosity more than anything else.

———

Lorne allowed Orlick to lead the way, not that it made very much difference. He, like her, would be following the hints on the retinal display.

The spots the foreman had marked out.

When Orlick came to a halt, he wore a grin. She knew that his mindset had shifted away from nervousness for the time being. That he was excited now.

She checked the timer and saw that they were almost through the first hour.

"We've got to get going," Lorne said. "We're running down the clock."

"Okay — do you mind going first?"

Lorne laid her drill on the ground before her. She tapped a few buttons. Through her helmet she could hear no sounds, but she imagined a mechanical whirr as the device retracted its drill from within its sturdy casing. The light on her retinal display was red while the drill prepared itself. The light then shifted to amber.

And finally go-ahead green.

She glanced at Orlick. "It really does all the work for you. All you have to do is set the trajectory. The degree of penetration."

Orlick watched with extreme concentration as Lorne whisked through the screens on her retinal display, her Link feeding the instructions back to the drill, delivering her orders.

Before long, she ordered the drill to commence.

Standing back, away to one side, they watched as the drill steered itself into the rock face, changing its angle in accordance with her commands. Its drill bit began to rotate. And then there was a hum passing through everything — passing through her suit — as it made contact with the rock.

When the drill had disappeared into the hole it had made, spitting out a trail of dust and debris into the tunnel as it went, she looked to Orlick and told him to have a go.

He picked out a spot — about fifteen, twenty paces away — and set his own drill going.

The two of them watched his drill disappear into the rock face just as hers had done.

About twenty minutes passed, the two of them in silence, monitoring their drills' progress through the cave on their retinal displays. An alert in her earpiece announced the SalDroids' arrival. Sure enough, she turned to see the SalDroids rounding the corner.

They were squat — close to the ground, coming up no higher than her shins. Each of them had a large chamber on their back, with enough capacity for about a ton of material.

Immediately they set about their work, following the trail of debris behind the drills.

The two of them soon disappeared into the holes.

"This feels like taking a dog for a walk," Orlick said.

Lorne tried her best to resist, but she found herself smiling at this remark. Soon, though, the smile was wiped off her face. Her Link was flashing a message at her:

Drill returning

She was fairly certain what that meant. Her drill had sustained damage. She scolded herself, thinking that if she hadn't had Orlick here to distract her she would have better analysed the route her drill was taking.

She would've studied the information on her retinal scanner better.

First the SalDroid backed up out of the hole. As always, it was covered with dust and grit. She could see that it wasn't much over a quarter full. Already, she could sense the upcoming reprimand from the foreman for damaging equipment.

It wasn't the first time it had happened.

Lorne thought about how they would debit her account to

cover the repair work. But when she no longer cared how much she had accumulated what did it really matter?

Orlick had come over to see what the fuss was about.

Silently, she wished he would mind his own damn business.

The drill backed out of the hole, its bit bent and twisted. That was no surprise. She supposed she had set a course direct for some bedrock. That was the result of a failure to pay proper attention.

"What've you got?" Orlick asked her.

Lorne glanced at her drill and decided there was no harm in sharing the details of her payload. In silence, the two of them watched as the summary appeared before their eyes on their retinal scanners. All the usual suspects until she reached the final item.

Rhodium.

Almost a kilo of it.

She looked at Orlick, trying to sense whether he understood what this meant.

He continued to stare at his retinal display, awaiting her interpretation.

Lorne thought this through. She knew that the foreman would have seen her results by now. That it would've been flagged up on his own Link, and that he would be viewing this breakdown at this very moment. As if on cue, she heard the foreman in her earpiece.

"Well, look what you've got there, Operative Gnoltes! Haven't seen anything like it in all my years. Guess there are some good reasons for busting a drill bit. Get your companion drilling that same spot right now! Just over an hour of window to go. I'd like to get some others in there with you, open up some more holes, but I don't think we've got time."

Lorne drew breath. She felt the mechanical tick of the oxygen tanks on her back. She glanced at Orlick, knowing the foreman was speaking to him, telling him what he had just told Lorne.

When she saw Orlick was through with his conversation, she spoke swiftly, knowing there wasn't much time to waste. "Order your drill out of the hole — then follow the coordinates I am about to send."

Orlick blinked rapidly. Then he did as he was told.

Lorne watched Orlick's drill emerge and then trundle into Lorne's excavation site. The foreman came back over their earpieces. "I'll be guiding this one, guys. It's my neck on the line. Don't worry, you'll get your share. I'll see to that. No heart attacks down there, okay?"

As Lorne watched Orlick's drill disappear into the hole, she held her breath. It was only when her Link warned of an "obstructed airway" that she remembered to carry on breathing.

She waited as time ticked away, as the drill went about its work. She found herself staring down at her own drill — now out of service and in need of repair.

Was there anything sadder than a broken tool?

Although it felt like a much shorter time, she realised they must've been waiting for half an hour or longer. It was then that the foreman spoke into their earpieces again.

"Okay — we're going to clear out. Proceed to the extraction point. SalDroids and drills will be right on your coat tails."

———

Lorne sat bolt upright on the bottom bunk in the cabin she shared with three other women. She stared out through the porthole to the asteroid as it became more and more distant. There didn't seem to be anything spectacular about it — and yet what they had found was unmatched anywhere else in the known universe. She knew the Company would seek to track the asteroid and set back down upon it as soon as possible ... just when that might be was difficult to say ... it would demand the right conditions — another window like today might not come along for several years.

There was a throbbing in her ears. She felt as if her skull was being squeezed like a sponge. She was glad there was nobody else in the cabin with her. She wanted to be alone now. But that wish wouldn't be granted for long.

"Operative Gnoltes — report to the foremen's offices."

Lorne hesitated.

Logically, she knew this had been coming ... how could it not?

And yet, she wanted to spread out time as long as she could manage.

In the end, though, she rose from her bunk, zipping her overalls all the way up to her throat. She made her way out into the corridor of the ship.

———

It was like living aboard a bombed-out shopping mall. That was what she thought to herself often. She knew that before the Company had acquired this ship it had been a pleasure cruiser. There was still a swimming pool, although most days the water had a scummy greenish tinge to it, and there were several missing tiles in the bottom.

She attempted not to notice Orlick but he caught her eye before she had a chance to evade him. He wore a wide grin. "Guess this really was a big haul, huh?"

Lorne felt a stab of anger as she turned over the stupidity of this question. Did he really have no idea about the scale of this thing? Just what they were dealing with? Just what trouble this had got them into ... had got *her* into? "I guess so."

They passed a security droid. It scanned their identification and approved their access.

Her retinal display marked the route forward with a curving arrow. It was leading them into one of the meeting rooms. The two of them stepped through the doorway.

There was a trio of foremen, heads bowed, examining read-outs on their retinal displays, issuing orders. Two male, one female. One of the aspects of being a foreman that Lorne knew she would never be able to grasp was how they kept watch over hundreds of miners at the same time. It was one of those jobs where you needed to have eyes in the back of your head. The foreman in the middle — the female, and clearly the one in charge — glanced up. "Please sit."

Lorne took her place and Orlick sat beside her. The chairs were much squashier — *plusher* — than the ones in the miners' communal areas. But that was to be expected.

They had the attention of all three foremen now.

A smile tweaked the corner of the female foreman's mouth. "Well, that was certainly a dramatic run, wasn't it?"

Lorne said nothing and she could feel Orlick trembling slightly in the chair beside her.

"You'll be pleased to hear that we've had the batch verified and the on-site readings were accurate. *Prudent*, if anything." She pouted, examining something on her retinal display. "Rhodium. Always impressive ... but in such quantities ..." She looked over Orlick before settling on Lorne — as if coming to the conclusion that she was the main culprit. "You are to be commended for your cool head. Even when your drill busted inside the pit. We've run the analytics and it doesn't look like we're going to be able to revisit the site this generation. No safety windows. Too risky."

Although Lorne had always tried to keep herself as far away from the administration issues of the Company as she could manage, she knew that somewhere in the bowels of the mothership there would be actuaries balancing the cost of the insurance for another landing on the asteroid versus the potential payout from the mining operation. She knew the liability had to be substantial for the Company to refuse to risk another operation.

"So," the female foreman continued, "that brings us to the question of the immediate future. The two of you."

The two foremen on either side of the female foreman seemed to come to attention, like a pair of guard dogs. Expecting conflict at any given second from here on out.

"As you well know, the conditions of Company Operative contracts states a fixed percentage of any outputs. Indeed, this is one of the central aspects which brings Operatives together to work in unison with the Company. However, there is also a provision under the contract for "within reasonable bounds". This is an allowance for any ... *unusual* gains resulting from an operation." She narrowed her eyes. "Do you see where I'm going?"

Lorne's heart thumped in her throat.

The female foreman nodded to one of the male foremen sitting beside her.

A document appeared on Lorne's retinal display. She scanned the title, "Compensational agreement for contract of services". She supposed the same document had been served to Orlick.

"You can take time to browse this before agreement, of course. And you shall have access to impartial legal advice before acceptance. The terms of the offer is at the bottom of the first section. Do you have any questions for the time being?"

Lorne made it to the bottom of the page. She saw the figure quoted there. The agreement that her contract with the Company would be terminated if she accepted the payout. She knew that although the amount quoted was substantial — more than ten years' worth of work — it paled in comparison with what she was actually due as per the terms of her contract. Even with that vague clause on "within reasonable bounds".

When she shifted Orlick a sidelong glance, she saw his eyes were wide, like a child taking in the sights of an orbital theme park for the first time.

"I have no questions," Lorne replied.

Orlick spoke up. "I ... is this saying that we will get this ... and then, that's it? We'll leave. It's all over?"

When the female foreman smiled it was with an almost maternal warmth. "In essence, that's correct. Not bad for a first shift?"

————

"So, what're you going to do with your share?" Orlick asked.

Lorne stared ahead at the off-white floor, walls and ceiling of the ship corridor. They had left the foremen's offices behind and they were back in the operatives section of the ship. Through the portholes, she made out the inky velvet of space and the pinpricks of stars punctuating the emptiness. "I'm ... I want you to take my share."

"What do you mean?"

"I'm going to stay. With the Company."

"I don't understand."

"I'll ask for another agreement to be drafted. I will waive my bounty on the payload. Request that it's transferred to you. Request continuation of my contract as an operative."

Orlick's forehead wrinkled in confusion. "But ... why?"

"I have my reasons."

"I think you're just overwhelmed. Not thinking clearly. To be honest, I'm overwhelmed. I thought this would be a steady way to build up a pile. I never expected to win the lottery."

Lorne breathed in deeply. She shook her head and looked out into space. "No, I want to stay here. I want to carry on. I ..."

"But there's so much to see in the universe!" Mixed in with the general sense of hysteria, there was a touch of reprimand to his voice. "You never have to work again — you never have to go down on another asteroid!"

Lorne said nothing.

Orlick covered his face with his hand. "Look, what about this, you go ahead with that agreement. Sign over your claim to me. I promise I'll put it to one side. If you change your mind then look for me. I'll give you my details. I won't touch it, I swear."

Even though Lorne had only recently met Orlick, she knew he was sincere in what he said. She had never been a "people person" but she could still sense that impossible-to-pin-down feeling of "trustworthiness" just as well as anybody else.

"Do what you will," she said. "But I want to do this."

"I ... don't understand. Think about it, at least. Take the legal advice. Maybe you'll see things another way."

Lorne took a few steps towards her dormitory. "Maybe." She half-expected Orlick to pursue her but he stayed put. Although she didn't look back, she was certain that he wore the same expression of pure disbelief.

She didn't want to explain to him.

She didn't want to explain to anybody.

She had her reasons for being in the Company — just like everyone else.

Why wouldn't they let her be?

When she returned to her bunk, she set about composing her response to the foremen. There would be no taking it back when she pressed send. Having something like this in writing was as good as having signed in blood.

This was her chance to escape.

No ... it was someone else's chance to escape.

CUL-DE-SAC

A spark leaped from the fire and landed on the back of Figoa's hand. For the first few moments, there was no sensation. Just numbness. Then warmth.

Finally pain.

She let out a throaty exhale, suppressing the natural shriek she knew would bring her mother running from the kitchen and into the back garden. She had turned ten only last month and she was making an effort to be more grown up.

She had to learn to look after herself.

She sank her teeth into her bottom lip and sucked in air, dampening the pain. She rubbed at the back of her hand. She peered down at the fledgling fire. It was not much more than dark smoke and flames the size of her fingernails but she felt a glimmer of pride about it.

A few days ago, she had been reading a book at school about survival in the wilderness. There had been an entire chapter devoted to making a fire. Ever since she had read the advice, she had been unable to shake the urge to try it out for herself. She had decided that tonight would be perfect. It was a long summer evening when flames wouldn't raise immediate attention due to the gently setting sun. Also, her mother was occupied in the kitchen, preparing dinner for the guests who were to visit that evening — people who worked with Figoa's father. And so she had slipped out of the side door of the house and entered the small wooded area at the end of their back garden. She had busied herself collecting dried leaves and twigs. She had even gathered a handful of pine cones.

She examined the back of her hand, seeing that there was a

sooty mark — red around the edges — where the spark had bitten her. She glanced down at the fire.

All the flames had extinguished.

Tiny puffs of smoke rose in the crisp autumn air.

She could tell from the way that the leaves, twigs and pine cones were now covered in a coat of ash that she had run out of fuel. That had been one of the main tips from the book. It was important to maintain a healthy supply of fuel.

She would have to remember that next time.

"Figgy! Figgy!"

Heat ran through her blood. She startled, spinning around in a way her mother would immediately identify as suspicious. When she did look around, though, she was glad to see her mother wasn't within sight. That was another thing that Figoa had to learn to deal with better. She couldn't allow herself to show she was frightened.

"Come in please!"

Figoa glanced back down at the smouldering smoke at her feet. She had read in the book that it was important to pour a bucket of water over a fire you were going to leave unattended. Or to extinguish it with some dirt.

Not wanting to venture back into the house and draw attention to herself by fetching a bucket of water, she took several handfuls of dirt and piled them on the dying fire until smoke no longer rose. She stared at the collection of twigs, leaves and pine cones and then bounded back up the garden to the house.

———

A stink of onions filled the whole kitchen. Figoa brought her sleeve up to cover her major airways — just like they were taught in school when they had practice fire evacuations. In the bright kitchen lights, Figoa realised that it was darker outside than it had seemed.

She wondered if her mother had seen any flames or smoke.

Her mother had her back to her, working away at the electric stove. Her red apron was tied into a loose knot around the back of her neck. Her skin sparkled with perspiration. There were three large pots bubbling away. An extractor fan hummed in the background. The whole scene made Figoa think of those urban witch stories she sometimes read.

"I've run a bath," her mother said, without turning. "Please go and get cleaned up. I've laid a dress on the bed for you. Put it on and then come and give me a hand."

Figoa felt a shred of outrage. It was a sense of rebellion she always had whenever her parents told her to do things in a matter-of-fact way. However, she was getting to the age when she was keen to show strangers that she wasn't a little girl any more. That she could behave like an adult when she needed to.

"Okay, Mum," Figoa replied, recalling that her hands were covered with dirt, and she probably reeked of smoke. This was an easy way out.

Once Figoa had got herself clean in the bath — cleansed the smoky smell from her hair and rinsed her filthy hands — she towelled herself dry in her bedroom, seeing that her mother had laid out a chestnut-brown dress on the bed. It had frills and buttons about the waist.

Her *least* favourite dress.

But — resisting the urge to slip into a childish tantrum — she put it on and went downstairs.

Back in the kitchen, the oniony stink had weakened. Her mother still had the extractor fan blowing on maximum. An alarm on the oven bleeped as her mother poured the water from one of the saucepans down the sink.

Figoa crossed the kitchen tiles and stopped the alarm.

"Thanks, dear," her mother said, concentrating fully on tipping the water out of the saucepan. "What time is it?"

Figoa glanced at the oven clock. "It's just gone seven."

Her mother finished up with the saucepan, and set it on the side. The way the steam rose up brought Figoa into mind of the tendrils of smoke out in the back garden. She could see why adults were always telling kids not to play with fire ... it *was* awfully tempting. Her mother brought the saucepan back over to the stove, then set it down on a low heat. She wiped her hands dry on the front of her apron and then patted them on the sides of her jeans. "I've got to go and get ready," she said. "They'll be here around seven thirty."

Figoa was always struck by her mother's reaction to these dinners. It made her think of those antelopes in the nature documentaries her dad liked them all to watch "as a family". Her mother's strong smooth neck reminded her of one of those antelopes. The way she was in a constant state of being startled. As if she expected a lion to come leaping out of the tall grasses at any moment.

Her mother gazed about the kitchen. "Figgy, please can you set the table. There are candles in the cupboard. If they arrive early will you help Daddy to serve them drinks?"

"Okay, Mum."

Her mother nodded to herself as if away on some other plane entirely. And then — as if returning suddenly — a smile sparked across her lips. "I think everything's ready. You'll be a good girl tonight, won't you?"

"Yes, Mum."

"Good," her mother replied, slipping her apron off over her head and disappearing out of the kitchen. Figoa waited for the sound of her mother's footfall on the staircase but it didn't come.

And then she reappeared in the doorway. She stepped up to Figoa, gave her a strong hug and a kiss on the top of the head. "I won't be long," she said, disappearing again.

———————

After she had set the table, Figoa located the candlesticks — with fresh white candles already pressed into their bases. She set them in the centre of the table. She wondered if her mother had wanted her to light them. She hadn't said anything about it. Upstairs, she could hear the shower going. There was no time to ask her now, was there?

It was almost twenty-five past seven. The guests would be here soon. Her mother would expect the candles to be lit. Figoa realised she had left the box of matches in the back garden, where she had started the fire. Acting quickly, she slipped into the garden, padded to the spot where she had lit the fire, and retrieved the box of matches from where it lay. When she returned to the house, the rush of water upstairs had switched off.

Still feeling itches of guilt from earlier, she struck a match and lit the candles. When she was finished, she savoured the flickering warm light. She glanced at the burn mark on the back of her hand, seeing that it had turned a shade of dark purple, like a bruise.

There was the scrubbing sound of a key in the front door.

Figoa startled. In her moment of panic, she had the urge to slip back out into the garden, to disappear into the falling darkness. But she stood her ground. Told herself that she needed to be a "big girl". She trod her way into the kitchen, and then the front hall. Through the front door passed her father — a beaming expression pressed upon his face — and their two guests for the evening. Two women.

Figoa held her breath as she looked them over. Both women

were over thirty, maybe even over forty. One of them wore a tight-fitting red dress. She had smooth red hair which was cropped just short of her shoulders. The other woman wore a charcoal suit, a white blouse with a wide collar popped up. Her hair was buzzed short. She wore glasses. There was the sense that they had been in the middle of a joke that had stopped short when they all laid eyes upon Figoa. She had the eerie sensation that they had been speaking about her.

"Well, good evening, ma'am," the lady in the dress with the red hair said.

"Hello," Figoa replied.

"Nice to make your acquaintance," the woman with the suit and buzzed haircut said.

Figoa shifted her attention to her father. As always seemed the case, he wore his work suit with a fedora hat pressed onto his balding head. Although he had never been a tall man, he looked as if he had physically shrunk standing beside these two. He took his hat off, hung it up on the coat rack. The way his gaze flipped between the three of them made Figoa feel nervous. "Fig," he said, "would you ask our guests if they would like anything to drink?"

The woman in the dress smiled widely. "I'll have a white wine, please."

The woman in the suit held Figoa's gaze in an unnerving manner. "Anything soft. No real preference."

As Figoa turned away to tend to the kitchen, she couldn't help thinking that the woman in the suit sounded a bit like a robot. She definitely preferred the woman in the red dress so far. She sifted through the cupboard, doing her best to divine which glasses her mother would present to guests. She served the white wine from an open bottle in the fridge. She also discovered some orange squash which she served for the woman in the suit.

Upstairs, she could hear her mother prancing back and forth, still getting ready. Figoa knew her mother would have become more urgent in her actions now she heard the guests had arrived. It was always the case. There never seemed to be enough time.

"What's happened to your hand?" the woman in the dress asked as Figoa passed her the glass of white wine.

Figoa cradled her hand in the other, as if she had forgotten about it completely. She eyed the bruised surface. "I bumped into something."

"Looks like a burn to me," the woman in the suit said.

Figoa felt a heat pass up her spine. How did she know?

As if she was reading her mind, the woman in the suit continued. "We work in a lab, with your dad. We often see burns. From chemicals, or from fire. I would say your one looks like your bog-standard fire burn." She flashed a sharp smile but it felt programmed — unnatural. "A boring burn."

Her father joined them, a glass of water in his hand. "Oh, Fig, you haven't been playing with fire, have you?"

Her nerves jangled. "No."

The woman in the red dress spoke up. "I'll bet it was while you were lighting these candles, wasn't it?"

Her heart bounced into her throat. Blushing, she managed a few nods. "Yes, that's right."

"You've got to be careful," the woman in the dress said. "Fire has a mind of its own."

———

Figoa's mother descended the stairs wearing a cream silk blouse over a pair of black trousers. There was a whole host of what Figoa recognised as forced smiles between the women and her mother. Combined with fake, enthusiastic tones of voice. It put Figoa in mind of the nursery at her school. She thought about how when parents dropped off their children, all of the adults involved — the nursery nurses, the parents — all spoke in that same cloying, happy-pitched tone. She wondered if this act was for her benefit.

Would they have interacted differently if she hadn't been present?

Figoa's mother had been busy cooking a pasta bolognese that evening. It was Figoa's favourite. She couldn't help but feel the tiniest itch of betrayal to think that her mother was cooking this dish for guests. As if it was too private for her mother to be serving to strangers. All this, though, was forgotten by the time Figoa sat at the table with her food in front of her.

She was glad to find that the grown-ups kept the conversation between themselves. There was nothing more annoying when she was with adults and they constantly wanted her to be "involved", with their questions about her favourite subjects at school, and what sports and other activities she enjoyed. She could tell that her mother, too, was glad that her father and the two women carried on their conversation about their work. In her mind's eye, Figoa imagined herself and her mother sitting alone at the table, a pair of ghosts sitting opposite one another, while her father and the two women conversed between themselves, oblivious.

When it was time for dessert to be served, she helped her mother tidy away the plates, and then stood by her side in the kitchen while her mother scooped balls of ice cream out of a tub and into bowls. It surprised her when her mother spoke up. She hadn't said anything throughout dinner. "Be careful with what you say around these women, Figgy. I don't trust them."

At first Figoa felt confusion. And then she felt a shockwave ripple through her stomach. She wasn't sure what to make of this. She thought about the conversation the women had had with her father throughout dinner. She tried to recall one aspect which might've been reason to arouse suspicion. But she couldn't remember anything in particular. To be honest, though, she had been more focused on her pasta than on the conversation.

Realising they were out of earshot of the table, and that in any case her father and the two women were engrossed in conversation, Figoa dropped her voice. "Why not?" she asked.

"It's just a feeling. You know your dad's work. Sometimes there are people ... people with strange ideas."

"What's strange about their ideas?"

"Did you hear what they said?"

"No."

There was one of those pauses which told Figoa that this was one of those times when an adult was attempting to figure out whether or not what they had to say next was age-appropriate for the child they were speaking to. Either her mother decided it was, or else she was in desperate need of someone — anybody — to speak to.

"They've been testing on human subjects."

" 'Humans' ?"

"Yes, you know, that's what Daddy does. That's what his work colleagues do."

"Like doctors?"

"Not exactly. They ... they don't necessarily make people better." Her mother flinched and she cast a swift glance off to the dinner table — but they were all still deep in conversation. "They don't necessarily *want* to make people better."

"Why not?"

"Because it's just what they do."

There was a snappiness to the reply. At first Figoa was taken aback because she took it as a reprimand. That was when her mother would most often use that tone of voice. However, she soon realised the truth. That her mother was afraid.

That she was asking for help.

But how was Figoa supposed to help? And what was she supposed to help *with*?

There was a peal of laughter from the dinner table.

Her mother flinched. Her reaction frightened her. Acting on instinct, she held out her hand. "Mum, I burned myself today."

"Oh?" her mother replied, cleaning the rim of the bowls of ice cream with a dishcloth. "Was it when you were lighting the candles?"

"No, I was starting a fire in the back garden. I read it in a book and I wanted to try. I'm sorry."

"You'll have to be more careful next time, won't you? Help me serve, please."

Figoa held her breath. She had expected her mother to be angry, but in truth she hardly reacted. Her mind was elsewhere. Figoa realised a few seconds later that she was *disappointed* her mother wasn't angry with her. It felt like an anti-climax.

She accompanied her mother back to the table, with the bowls of ice cream.

———

"What do you think of that, Figoa?"

Figoa blinked to herself, returning to the present. She was still sat at the table, her bowl of ice cream finished before her. She had drifted away somewhere else. In truth, she had been thinking about the book which had taught her to make fire. She had wondered what else she might be able to gather from it. There were all sorts of survival skills within.

It was the woman in the dress who had spoken. When she turned her attention onto her, she saw she was smiling — that she was wearing one of those smiles brought on by the warm glow of wine and candlelight.

"What do I think?" Figoa asked.

"Yes, you know, about having something in your head." The woman tapped her temple as if Figoa was unsure which part of the body the head was. "It will connect you to everything. You'll have access to all manner of information straight away."

"I ... don't know."

"It'll be like your own personal super power. Won't that be fun?"

"I guess so."

Figoa's gaze shifted to her mother sat opposite. She was sitting with her eyes averted, straightening the table mat. Figoa knew that more than anything her mother was waiting for a lull in conversation so she could take away the empty bowls and return to the kitchen. But Figoa also knew that her mother wanted to take her with her.

"Has your daddy told you about what we do at work?"

Figoa glanced over the table at her father. He gave her a slight smile. There was something slightly nervy in his expression — something which caught her off guard. It looked as if he wasn't completely in control.

She shook her head.

"Well, we're experimenting with this technology. Practising putting these devices inside of minds. This will be the breakthrough of the century. Of all human history, perhaps. Would you like to be part of it?"

Here, Figoa noticed her mother become agitated. To begin with, Figoa thought that she might say something, but — instead — she rose to her feet. "Can I have your bowls, please?" she asked, and then went around the table collecting them up.

She expected her mother to make some subtle gesture for her to leave the table too, but she averted her gaze. She slipped away from the table, into the kitchen.

The woman in the dress continued as if nothing had happened at all. "Tell me, Figoa, what would you like to be when you grow up?"

"I haven't thought about it much."

"A doctor? A lawyer? A scientist?"

"Okay."

"And what if I said that this technology we are developing could very well aid you into any career of your choosing?"

"Okay."

Figoa looked to the kitchen again. There was a thunk as her mother dumped the bowls in the sink and then the sound of her mother climbing the stairs. She wondered where she was going. Had she heard her mother sob?

"Would you like to come and see the lab some day?"

Figoa turned her attention onto her father. She saw that he was staring at her intently. There was something she didn't like about his expression. A kind of detachment. As if he was watching this scene take place from a distance.

She shrugged. "All right."

"Then it's settled," the woman in the dress said, giving Figoa's father a smile. "We'll set up a date for the next week or so."

"Remember, Fig, it's your choice," her father said. "You're just coming to see what we do. There's no need to say yes or no to anything just yet."

When Figoa eyed the woman in the suit — who had remained silent throughout this conversation — she felt a shudder pass through her chest. It was the way the woman sat staring intently at her from beneath her glasses.

"You will be a great help," the woman in the dress said. "Because of regulations it's very difficult to find volunteers. To get parents to sign off on behalf of their children. In fact, I would say that if we can't find *someone* before too long then the whole project might be in trouble. We would greatly appreciate it."

"Daddy," she said, turning to her father. "Is this something that will hurt? If I ... do it?"

"No," he replied. "It won't hurt. It will be painless. Harmless. We're all quite sure."

The woman in the dress spoke again. "Your daddy would never do anything to hurt you, would he, Figgy?"

She felt a ticklish sensation in her chest. She wanted to cough to see if she could loosen the feeling. But she didn't want to make any sudden movements.

She thought she could hear sobbing upstairs. Her mother in the bedroom. Why had she gone away? Why had she left Figoa here with her father and his work colleagues?

She felt a slight sting on the back of her hand from where she had burned herself. She glanced to her father. "May I be excused?"

Her father beamed back. "Of course, dear."

———

Upstairs, Figoa crept across the landing, stopping outside her mother and father's bedroom. The door was cracked slightly open. She could see her mother sitting on the edge of the bed. Her head in her hands.

Figoa didn't want to disturb her. She wanted to go to her bedroom and close the door.

Downstairs, she could hear her father banging about the kitchen, preparing coffee for his colleagues. They would be gone soon. Why didn't her mother go back down to join them?

Her mother straightened up, peeling her hands away from her

face. She looked at Figoa through tear-soaked eyes. She gestured her inside.

Figoa held back a few moments. Unsure about herself. And then she did as her mother wanted. She sat on the bed beside her, feeling her reassuring warmth and weight.

Her mother wrapped her arms about her.

After a few moments, Figoa spoke up. "Mum? Do I have to do this?"

"Your father wants you to. He says it's safe. It would really help him to get ahead. It would help us. And he thinks it would help you too."

"Help me how?"

"Like they said, you'll have access to so much information. You will be able to do whatever you want."

"Like not go to school?"

"You'll still have to go to school ... but you'll be different. *Special.*"

Figoa thought about this for a moment. She wasn't sure she wanted to be special. And she was absolutely certain she didn't want to be *different*.

"What do you think?" Figoa asked.

Her mother breathed in deeply, then she looked to the bedroom door. Figoa half expected her mother to break down into tears again. But she remained strong. Her voice didn't show any signs of cracking. "I think they have good intentions. Mostly. But I don't want to see you get hurt. Or damaged in any way."

Again, Figoa thought of the burn on the back of her hand. She wondered if her mother had some camomile lotion she could rub on it to make it feel better — to take the sting out of the burning sensation.

"I won't do it unless you say it's okay," Figoa said.

Her mother sat staring at the door.

Downstairs, Figoa could hear her father still speaking in dampened tones with his work colleagues. She imagined that they each had a cup of coffee now. She caught whiffs of the smell floating up the staircase.

"I trust your father. I *love* your father."

Figoa realised her mother hadn't answered the question.

Her mother got to her feet. "Come on," she said, holding out her hand. "We need to be getting back down to the others. They'll be wondering where we've gone."

Figoa held back a second. She knew she had to ask questions. That there was so much that had gone unsaid. But she felt paralysed — numb.

As her mother's fingers clasped hers, and they trod their way back downstairs, she felt the sting of the burn at the back of her hand. What had once been a searing heat was now no more than a throbbing annoyance. Perhaps tomorrow she wouldn't feel anything at all.

It would become normal.

She guessed it would be the same with this procedure she would undergo.

Discomfort.

And then it would heal.

NOTHING PAINTED WHITE

A blank piece of white card lay on Customs House Manager Appardly Dhankston's desk. He flipped it over expecting there to be something on the other side.

But there was nothing.

He glanced back over his shoulder, flipping his thinning, greying, shoulder-length hair as he did so. He had expected to see someone standing watching, grinning to themselves. Their idea of a joke. He knew that his reputation throughout the office was that he was a neat freak. In truth, he was someway beyond mere neat-freakdom. He would go as far as to say that he was a neo-minimalist. Everything must go.

There was no one else in the colony customs offices yet. As was always the case, he was the first to arrive. He had been the one to flip on the lights. If somebody *had* left this card on his desk as some sort of misinformed joke then they hadn't bothered to get up early to come and see the reaction.

He crunched the card into a ball in his fist and tossed it into the waste paper basket behind his chair. He didn't much like seeing anything in the waste paper basket but he was hardly going to go fish it out and drop it in another bin just because of his OCD.

The cleaning droid would be by soon enough to empty it.

Appardly hung his long coat up on the wall hook and then raised his desk — via his frontal lobe link — so that he could comfortably stand. He had always been tall and it seemed a waste to be sitting hunched over himself all day. He had to use all of the natural advantages he had. Goodness knew he had never had so much as a muscle on his entire body. He had always been the lankiest boy at school.

Once he had engaged his Link, he examined the Migh-Honey

Colony map which hung down over the entire wall. When he looked over it with his retinal scanner, the colony rose into a three-dimensional, real-time representation. All of the traffic moving at that moment in time. If he so wished, he could zoom in on any one aspect — such as a transport — and an identification tag would appear giving him the surname and personal reference of the registered owner.

Beside the colony map, there was a map of the entire planet — Ganbe — as seen from outer space. When he used his Link on this map he saw a real-time vision of all outer-space traffic. As with the colony map, each ship had an identification tag giving basic details of the registered owners.

Satisfied that traffic looked unremarkable this morning, Appardly turned his attention to his desk, having his retinal display project his inbox onto the surface. A hundred or so messages awaited his attention. He tried to read the first one.

But found he couldn't take his mind off the piece of card.

He turned.

Saw it there.

Neatly crunched into a ball.

Sitting at the bottom of the bin.

He held himself still for several seconds. He knew it would be a victory for whoever had been responsible for leaving the card on his desk if he got riled about it ... but there was getting riled about it and getting *riled* about it. He was just trying to keep his mind clean.

Because — after all — a clean mind was a focused mind.

Again glancing about the office to ensure nobody was observing him, Appardly bent over and retrieved the piece of white card crunched into a ball. As he trod across the office, towards the bin over by the front door — well out of sight and therefore out of mind — something occurred to him. He stopped.

Uncrunched the ball of card. Allowed it to unfurl in his palm. He engaged his retinal scanner.

Sure enough, it was as he had suspected.

There was something there.

Hidden from normal vision but unlocked by virtual reality.

It was an intricate woven pattern. All swirling lines and inter-locking shapes.

A sort of abstract monogram.

What did it mean?

The creased card gave topography to the design. Lifting it into being a three-dimensional object. Appardly stretched his mind, hoping to realise where he had seen this before ... *if* he had seen this before. It was certainly familiar.

He returned to his desk with the cardboard. Gazed at its smooth lines. He felt a sudden stillness to be considering the design. There was something about puzzles which always calmed him.

"Morning sir."

Appardly startled. Glanced up.

It was Terri — his personal assistant. She was around twenty years old — a good thirty years younger than he was. Her hair was naturally a chestnut colour, or at least that was the colour it had been when he had taken her on six months ago, but now it was pink. He had done his best to have that rectified, but she had neatly, deftly — *cheerfully* — defied him at every stage of the human-resources led process he had attempted to initiate.

"Do you know anything about this?" he asked, holding up the piece of card.

Terri squinted. "What is it? A blank piece of paper?"

"No, try scanning it."

She reached for the card. "Oh, I see now."

This was one of those traits that he most abhorred in Terri.

How she always wanted to touch — *feel* — anything and everything. Appardly reluctantly released the card.

"You think it's some kind of marketing?"

"Possibly. I don't know. Is it familiar to you? It was lying on my
desk. Do you know who left it there?"

She glanced up. "No, sir, everything was immaculate when I
left last night. And you left after me, if you remember?"

Appardly did remember. He made it a point of principle not
only to be the first to arrive everyday but also to be the last one out
of the door. He supposed he was lucky in a way that he lived
alone, that he had no close relatives or family on the colony. He
could dedicate himself completely to his work.

"Did you check the surveillance footage?" Terri asked, with a
shrug, handing the card back to him, and then heading off to the
women's toilets to do whatever it was she did for five minutes there
every morning.

Appardly scolded himself for having neglected such a simple
thing. But then he reminded himself that he had only uncovered
the card's secret moments earlier. The piece of card had been
swiftly upgraded from "rubbish" to "potentially useful object".

As Customs House Manager, he had access to the entire
surveillance system surrounding the offices. He ordered playback
now through his retinal display, spinning the vantage point around
so that his desk would be in centre stage.

He watched as the clock at the bottom corner of his retinal
display swept around eight-times faster than real-time. He
watched himself go about his day in a sort of slapstick fashion.
Standing for long periods at his desk before inevitably being inter-
rupted by someone, leading to a period of high-speed nodding, the
odd flailing arm before he returned to his spot.

He slowed the footage as it got towards the end of his working
day.

Although he was focused upon his work station, he sensed the rest of the office slowly emptying out before leaving him alone. A kind of chill seized his gut. He banished the feeling with a hard swallow.

The clock was nearing half seven when he watched himself relinquish his desk. It was usually when his stomach started to grumble.

When his body began to fail him.

Demanding sustenance and sleep.

On the footage, he stretched his arms up to the ceiling — a gesture which he would never in a million years allow his employees to observe him partaking in — then he slipped his jacket on over his shoulders and trudged out of the office.

Appardly zoomed in closer on his desk. It was spotless. He watched the clock. Seeing the time come up to nine, and then ten ... *eleven*.

Just before midnight, there was movement.

He slowed playback.

Focused on the image.

But he failed to understand what he saw.

It was a young child — perhaps eight, nine years old. At least he *thought* it was a child. It was near impossible to tell because they were covered from head to toe in a onesie.

Tiger stripes.

It looked as if this child had been dropped off at a friend's birthday party.

He watched the child lay the card down on his desktop. Just as he had seen it this morning when he had come in. As he watched the child retreat across the office, he attempted to request identification. His Link gave him an immediate response:

No identification found

Appardly retreated from the footage, bringing the real world back to full brightness from where it had lain in near darkness in the background of his retinal display. He saw Terri was on the other side of the office now. Making his morning coffee. He had to admit one thing — she certainly understood how he operated. She knew how to ebb in and out of his rituals seamlessly. Perhaps it was for the best that she had stuck around.

As Appardly made his way back to his desk he knew that the biggest question was just how that child had managed to gain access to the building. And at that time of night.

There must be some explanation.

Appardly returned to his desk, deciding to make a start on sifting through his mailbox. As he did so, he kept careful track of the office arrivals, although they were so predictable — so in keeping with every other day — that he wondered why he bothered.

First there was Maureen, his Fraud Investigator, and then there was Kenji, who was in charge of Fauna and Flora Imports. As he spotted these key arrivals, other worker bees floated in, looking as if they lacked direction or agency. Appardly had to remind himself that he had once been like them, back when he had started. And then — last as always — was Lowanna, his Head of Narcotics Enquiries.

Whenever Lowanna arrived late — today at seven minutes past ten — Appardly felt the same tightness in his chest. He knew that the rest of the office was judging him. That the rest of the office was waiting to see how he would react ... if he would take any kind of action. As always, Lowanna wore a beaming smile as she rolled herself in her wheelchair past the other workers. Today she had on a deep purple dress and wore her hair in plaits. A pinch of fury twisted in his gut to think that she had had time to get up and make herself presentable.

Why hadn't she thought to organise herself sufficiently to arrive on time?

At the beginning, he had allowed for Lowanna's tardiness because of her disability. He had been afraid that it might be the reason for her late arrivals. However, when he had eventually approached her about the issue — in a tender, gentle manner — she had apologised profusely and promised that she would make more of an effort to keep time in future. And for about a week she had. Then she had slipped back into the same old routine.

Habits died very hard.

Even worse was the effect she had on the other workers. As she passed them by, they returned her smile. How had he managed to employ a narcotics officer who was actually *likeable*? He thought back to Oliver Anderson, the previous post holder. He had been a tough old boot. He certainly had made no friends here, but he was always in the office minutes after Appardly. There had been one or two occasions when he had actually arrived a few *seconds* earlier than Appardly himself. Worse of all, though, was that Lowanna was quite possibly the most brilliant employee he had ever had. Seizures of unauthorised merchandise had gone through the roof ever since he had taken her on. And he had to admit to himself that the special commendation he had received this time last year from Colony Chief Gomez had been very much influenced by this. Gomez had admitted it to him herself.

"Morning, boss," Lowanna said, in that low, purring voice of hers.

Appardly did his best to conceal his inner rage at her carefree attitude to her lateness. "Good morning. I have something for you to look at." He led her over to his desk, and to the piece of cardboard there. He saw that Terri had left his coffee there too, and he picked it up and took a swig. A touch bitter. That was how he liked it.

There was no point in having everything your own way in this life.

Lowanna held the piece of cardboard, pouting to herself as she turned it over.

Appardly said nothing. He just watched beyond the rim of his mug.

Waiting.

He wanted to see just how *brilliant* Lowanna truly was.

Part of him wondered whether disability bestowed the sufferer with especially acute awareness in another part. That old chestnut about God never closing a door without opening a window, or however it went. They said it about the blind most often. How as a result of living in perpetual darkness they were forced to develop their other senses.

To gain a keener sense of smell, hearing, touch, taste.

Did the same hold true for a paraplegic?

He observed as Lowanna's gaze became unfocused. As her eyes slipped back into her skull and she went miles away as she scanned it with her retinal display.

It irked Appardly to think that it had only occurred to him to scan the piece of card several minutes after discovering it. Perhaps Lowanna was especially insightful.

"Well?" Appardly asked after a few moments.

"It's a dealer mark of some kind." Lowanna blinked several times and her gaze returned to normal. She set the piece of card back on Appardly's desk. "But I've never seen this particular design before."

"Nothing in the files?"

"No, I checked."

"No connections to anything at all?"

"Not that I can see."

There was a pause.

"What? What is it?" Appardly asked.

"There is a certain similarity to another dealer's mark."

"Who?"

"The Huntharn Collective."

Appardly thought long and hard. He had a peripheral knowledge of dealers. He didn't need to have anything more. His role only required him to have an awareness of everything. To know which of his employees was the specialist in every area.

Who he should be holding accountable.

"Is there anyone we can go see for information?"

"I have a few contacts."

That was another thing which sat ill with Appardly. How Lowanna was a people person. She was able to strike up a conversation with anyone and everyone. Make them feel at ease. Appardly's professional sense of pride stood in direct conflict with the very idea that they should be on friendly terms with the enemy ... even if it did yield excellent results.

Appardly made his mind up. "There's something about this one I don't like. Not at all. This piece of card ended up on my desk. It was brought into the office in the dead of night. By a *child*."

Lowanna said nothing.

"Does that bring you into mind of anything you've seen?"

"No," she replied. "It doesn't."

Her response was so quick Appardly had no time to judge whether or not she was really telling him the truth. He suspected — on more than one occasion — Lowanna had held back on the true extent of her connections to the criminal community on Migh-Honey Colony.

———

Light from the nearest star — Osiris — streamed through the Bubble protecting the colony capital. Although the light from Osiris was a ruby red colour, the Bubble offset this, giving it a warm Earth-orange tint. The Bubble provided the colony with an artificial ozone layer, allowing the colonists to live out their lives in an otherwise normal — *Earthlike* fashion — on a planet far away from their home world. Appardly often wondered if he might visit Earth one day. Those who did always talked it up as a "spiritual" experience. As if they had been dreaming of the place their entire life. The cynic in him always wondered just how much of it was nostalgia. Earth was a dried-up husk careening through its death spiral.

Appardly watched the buildings slip by the transport window. He was conscious of Lowanna sitting across from him. She was reading information off her retinal display. Reading up on the case. He wished that he might be able to reprimand her for something or other ... but it was too late for him to speak about her tardiness this morning — the moment had gone — and there was no other element of her work performance which was lacking.

But most of all, he didn't want to disturb her.

He had the inkling that they were on the cusp of something big.

The transport came to a halt in the Fernridge Neighbourhood. An area of the city Appardly had only heard of from reputation. He hadn't doubted they would end up somewhere like this, though, and he glanced across to Lowanna, glad to allow her to give him the cues for a change.

Feeling strangely redundant, he stood to one side as the ramp on the transport engaged, and Lowanna wheeled her way down it. "We have an appointment with the Veena family."

Appardly felt a chill creep into his blood. "The Veenas?" he replied. "As in Eli Veena?"

He thought of the case — three or four months ago — when they had caught Eli Veena with a whole ship full of a prohibited substance. Something they called "clay" on the streets. The quantity suggested it was a supply intended for multiple planets, and the lack of any attempt to disguise the shipment spoke of an arrogance Appardly did not see very often.

In fact, he had taken it as an insult.

As Appardly followed Lowanna through an entrance into a large apartment building, he glanced up the street as if Colony Chief Gomez might be keeping a personal eye on him.

Checking out his credentials.

The truth, of course, was that Colony Chief Gomez didn't need to be on the same planet to check up on his whereabouts. She could consult with her Link anywhere in the universe.

Appardly hoped anyone examining his movements wouldn't tie his current location to the criminality of the Veenas ... as much as the sniff of corruption around the Customs House Manager was often the death knell.

They gained security clearance for the building and entered the lift. The doors slid shut and the mechanical hum surrounded them as they rose. "Remember that Eli is the only criminal in the family," Lowanna said.

"The only *convicted* criminal," Appardly added with a murmur.

They arrived on the fifteenth floor, where the Veena residence commenced, occupying the next five floors, including the penthouse.

Appardly had to admit he admired their gall. They were shameless in how they presented themselves. They hid in plain sight. He wondered if it was some kind of genius, and then he thought about Eli Veena and wondered if it wasn't just bull-minded arrogance and a whole heap of luck.

The Veenas had their own personal security detail. The security check was far more thorough than the one at the building entrance. As they ran their scanners over him, and then gave him a pat-down, Appardly did his best not to utter some rehash of the phrase, "Don't you know who I am?"

They were shown up into a room hanging with what Appardly hoped — for the sake of his pride — were glass beads rather than diamonds. There was a large window which took in a landscape view of the colony capital. In the distance, he could make out the steady arc of a shuttle leaving the spaceport, sailing up into the heavens. Even now, as a jaded adult, he still held a kind of child-like wonder for space travel. At one point he had wanted to be a captain. It made him smile ... until he realised he was daydreaming and the real world — his actual circumstances — caught up with him.

One of the walls in the room was a mural. It depicted a sunset in a desert, complete with golden paint. The sweeping sand dunes reminded Appardly of ocean waves. Of the waves he would see in films and virtual-reality representations of Earth.

There was an elderly woman sitting on a wooden chair in the centre of the scene. Her head bowed to her chest as if she might have dozed off. She wore a robe wrapped about her shoulders, a scarf coiled up around her throat. Appardly wondered if she didn't feel a little hot. He was sweating from just the few steps he had taken from the Veenas' security area. The desert scenery wasn't helping much.

"Appardly Dhankston — Customs House Manager."

"Lowanna Hearth — Narcotics Investigator."

The elderly woman spoke quietly. "It is a little warm in here, isn't it?"

Appardly felt taken aback for a second. He could swear the woman had read his mind.

As if the woman had uttered a silent command, the room shifted. The walls changed from the desert to an icy landscape. One which reminded Appardly of the South Pole back on Earth. He felt a chill about his collar. And then a full-on icy blast. Before he could get his thoughts straight, he was almost knocked off his feet by the searing wind. When he felt his stability returning, he realised that Lowanna had reached out and taken hold of the front of his shirt, preventing him from falling flat on his back.

"Maybe a little too much," the woman muttered.

The world around them again shifted. This time it became a placid lake scene. Low, rolling hills. An overcast sky. Moist air with a slight smell of rain.

Appardly looked to Lowanna. He was somewhat disappointed to find that she was unmoved by this display. He did his best to compose himself, turning his attention back onto the elderly woman. She had straightened up now. He could make out her face. Her creased features. How she peered out at them through pinched eyes. He had a hard time not picturing her as a cartoonish witch. "We've come regarding an investigation," he said. "We were hoping you might be able to shine some light on a matter."

It seemed as if the woman was peering right through him. It was an uncomfortable feeling. It felt as if he was completely exposed. "Is that so?" she said.

"Lowanna?"

Lowanna wheeled herself toward the woman and offered her the card.

The woman took it from her, holding it in her hands. She breathed in deeply, her birdlike shoulders rising and falling. Her gaze remained fixed on the piece of card for an unnaturally long time.

"Well?" Appardly asked. "Anything?"

Lowanna shot him a fiery look — a look which Appardly was unaccustomed to being on the receiving end of from a subordinate.

"It's a mark," the woman said.

"Yes, we know that," Appardly replied. "But whose mark is it?"

"An imitation. It should belong to the Huntharn Collective but ..." she indicated the card with her bony finger and Appardly activated his retinal display so that he might see the hidden design "... you see this, around here, I would say that this is a different element. It is nothing currently in circulation."

"A 'knock-off', to use the vernacular?" Appardly put in.

"No," the woman replied. "Only unique. And technically not property of the Huntharn Collective."

"Then who would've done it?"

The sky surrounding them became gloomier. Clouds were closing in overhead. Appardly was certain he felt a few spots of rain on his cheeks.

"The wrong question," the woman said.

"Why would they have done it?" Lowanna put in.

"That's more like it."

Again Appardly cursed Lowanna for her ease with the criminal element based on the colony. He hated this. He *hated* giving control to his own subordinates, let alone to the criminal elements they were supposed to be opposing.

"Then *why?*" Appardly asked.

As if he was being punished for being overly forthright, a fat rain drop landed in the centre of his scalp. It was freezing cold. He felt its impact send a shudder through his bones.

"A warning," the woman said.

Appardly glanced to Lowanna. He had the uneasy feeling that she and the woman were on one side, or at the very least had a private understanding. He wanted her to take the lead from here on out.

"The card was brought to us by a child," Lowanna said. "We checked the surveillance footage. The card was left on my boss's desk. Who were they trying to warn? Us, Colony Authorities? The Huntharn Collective?"

"The Huntharn Collective."

"And to warn them against what?" Lowanna continued.

"Meddling with shipments."

This time Lowanna glanced at Appardly and he was glad to see that she also wore a look of exasperation. So it wasn't only him who was growing uneasy with the stilted flow of information. "But how would we know which shipments?"

"The sign. Anything with the sign."

Appardly looked at the card again. The dealer's mark there. And he wondered just what he was getting himself in for.

———

"Over here, boss. Take a look!"

Appardly followed Lowanna's voice. He had to duck to avoid the low-hanging pipes in the storage bay of the ship they were inspecting.

When he had got back to the office, he had decided to play it safe — to personally inspect the cargo on every ship that passed in and out of the colony port. He didn't like mysteries. And he categorically *hated* playing games. Which was all this whole escapade amounted to.

He wanted this thing sorted out.

Without fuss.

And without any damage to his reputation.

Lowanna had come across a large, unremarkable-looking crate.

And he immediately saw that it bore the dealer's mark. The mark which the woman had decided was a "warning".

Appardly ordered a droid along to transport the crate down onto the dock for inspection. Just to be safe, he contacted Colony Security, requesting full back up. They complied with the request, giving him a pair of officers who stood at the ramp up to the ship's entrance, hands hovering over their blaster grips.

The ship captain was remarkably calm. Usually they got riled during inspections. Everything that was on board would ultimately be the captain's responsibility. The captain would be the one who would need to answer questions — and be liable for penalties — if the load was found to be illegal.

Appardly looked to Lowanna, beside him, as if challenging her to tell him not to go ahead. But although her eyes betrayed her worry, she remained silent. And he knew he had to go ahead with the inspection. It was his job to take action.

The droid worked on the crate, cracking it open with its hydraulic arm. One of the officers peered over as the droid worked. There was always something infinitely interesting about cracking open deliveries. You were never quite sure what you would uncover.

The lid fell onto the port with a slap of wood against concrete.

Appardly held back a moment and then paced forward. He stood at the side of the crate. Peered within. What he saw inside took his breath away.

It was a child.

Just as he had done in the surveillance footage, the child wore a tiger onesie.

There was nothing else in the crate.

The child appeared to be sleeping. His eyelids sealed. A gentle rosiness to his cheeks.

"Jesus," Appardly uttered, then — shouting out, "Get Child Services!"

———

Appardly sat bolt upright at his desk, scanning his inbox, although it was impossible to make sense of any of the messages scrolling before his eyes. He kept on glancing around, to the child sitting in the room off to one side of the office. Lowanna was seeing to him. She was good with children — he knew she was a mother.

Shortly after they had opened the crate and he had laid eyes on the child within, the child had begun to cry. He could still recall the sense of panic which'd swept through him. Although he had never been a father, he knew that there had been a hint of the paternal about those feelings. Some deeper sense warning him about a threat to the child.

Urging him to help protect the species.

Lowanna wheeled herself out of the office, leaving the child behind. She rolled over to Appardly's desk. "I can't get anything out of him," she said. "Seems like he's been traumatised by something."

"He's the same kid as on the video feed, isn't he?"

"He's wearing the same costume ... but you can't make out the face on the footage."

Appardly thought on this. His attention drifted onto the surveillance video which had showed the child in the tiger onesie laying the seemingly blank piece of card on his desk.

Where had the child gone afterward?

He had no access to that information, of course. Once anything went outside of that office door, it became the remit of Colony Security.

Appardly returned to the scene, to Lowanna sitting before him. "I keep thinking of the dealer's mark. That woman — "

"Helena Veena."

"She told us that the dealer's mark was a warning to the Huntharn Collective. Not a warning directed at us, the Colony Authorities ..."

"Because they don't see us as a threat. We don't have the funding to *really* come down hard on anyone."

Although Appardly acknowledged the truth of this statement, he felt a slight burning sensation in his chest. Perhaps he disliked one of his employees weighing in on higher-level strategy. He wondered if deep down he was concerned about one of them coming for his job.

"The dealers, then. This Huntharn Collective. They were the ones being warned off from meddling. I assume they would have the resources to cause issues with these shipments?"

Lowanna nodded.

"Is there anyone we can talk to about it?"

Lowanna sighed. "The Veenas were my best bet."

"You have no other contacts?"

"No. You might call the Huntharn Collective hard to pin down."

"In what way?"

"Well, they aren't a family operation, as is often the case. They have no set central base either. Not one that we know about. They use freelancers. People without ties. And they don't leave a trail."

"Not like the Veenas," Appardly replied, again thinking of Eli Veena, and the sheer bullheadedness with which he had conducted himself in getting caught. "The Huntharn Collective operate on the sly. What does that mean?"

"It means that they don't want to threaten their operations with bold power statements."

"They're serious about what they do."

"Or there are serious consequences of getting caught."

"The sort of consequences which might attract Interstellar Police attention?"

"That's what I'm thinking."

Appardly thought back to the mark again. "So whoever is creating these knock-off marks is treading on the toes of the Huntharn Collective. And they are attempting to ward them off. They're also doing something sufficiently large so that only authorities with great scale, great power — illicit or otherwise — would be able to stop them."

Lowanna seemed lost in thought for several seconds. When she blinked back to the present her eyes appeared almost hollow. "Do you ever feel like you're out of your element?"

Appardly didn't respond, turning to see a personal transporter glide into place outside and a pair of Child Services officers disembark.

———

"Genuinely the weirdest thing I've ever seen."

Appardly eyed the Child Services officer — a woman in her fifties with a puff of greying curly hair and rosy cheeks. She wore a fuzzy red jumper which brought out the blush in her complexion. He was showing her the ship in which the child had arrived.

"Third one in a week," she said. "We picked up the other one yesterday. Same clothing. Same tiger onesie. And now this ..."

"What'd you mean?"

"Twins ... *triplets*, I suppose, now there're three of them. Identical. All of them about as verbose as the other."

"They don't say anything either?"

"Not word one. Not even their names. We have given them all

a name just to call them something." The woman sighed. "What about the captain? I imagine Colony Security have taken him in?"

"Yeah."

The woman sighed a second time. "Then we'll have to make do with their reports. Sometimes we get lucky — we get a chance to ask our own questions. But not if Colony Security get there first."

Appardly smirked.

The woman exchanged a smile. "I guess you've got your own bug bears with Security, huh?"

"Let's just say we do our best to stay out from under their feet." He thought to himself. And then made up his mind. He fingered the dealer's mark on the side of the crate. "Do you recognise this?"

"Huntharn Collective," the woman replied, without missing a beat. "We get a whole bunch of kids with it carved on their arm."

"Apparently it's not quite theirs. In fact, it's quite clever. Something about the design is giving a warning."

The woman pouted. "Hmm, I'm no expert. I just go on whatever I hear. On what I see."

"Is there anything that might help us out at Child Services?"

The woman remained very still. She appeared to be looking at the dealer's mark, inspecting it more closely, but Appardly knew she was considering the question. Wondering just how she should respond. Attempting to work out whether he was a threat or not. Appardly knew how women acted around children — how protective they were of them even if they weren't their own.

Especially when they weren't their own.

She straightened up. "Maybe," she replied. "Maybe not. Do you think that's the key to finding out where these shipments come from?"

"Like you said, Colony Security aren't likely to allow us to ask the captain questions. And I reckon he'll be in a hurry to get away from here when he's released. There'd be no reason for him to talk to us."

———

Appardly did his best to check his stiff, tense posture on the way across the colony with the woman from Child Services — or Hattie, as she had asked him to call her. He forced himself to relax his shoulders, to rest his palms flat on his thighs.

Hattie herself was also clearly racked by nervous tension.

Her gaze flitted at objects passing them by outside the window. The slightest bump in the road caused her to sit up straight and look around as if she was being stalked by an invisible predator. Lowanna and the other Child Services officer — the child himself, still wearing his tiger onesie — sat at the other side of the transport.

The Bubble was beginning to fade the light, although Osiris would continue to burn brightly, not setting for another forty Earth days. Without the Bubble, the ensuing forty days, once Osiris had set, would have meant freezing temperatures and pitch blackness. However, when Osiris did slip beneath the horizon, the Bubble would continue to power the colony using energy farms on the other side of the planet. Keeping the colony constantly powered-up — well-lit during the days and in a twilight haze during the nights.

They arrived at Child Services at around five in the evening. Child Services had been styled as a kind of tumbledown country house picked up and plonked into the middle of an urban setting. He had to admit that they had been successful to a degree. There was an undoubtedly homey quality to the place ... something extremely hard to achieve given the building's function of providing temporary sanctuary for children victim of all manner of tragedies.

Lowanna disappeared off into the registration area with the child and the other Child Services officer. Meanwhile Hattie led Appardly through the building. She guided him with the surety of someone who had worked — and lived — in the place for a long time. He recognised the qualities from his own work. He knew that such knowledge created a kind of foundation and structure for the rest of his life. Work gave everyone a steady, unmoving touch-stone from which everything else flowed.

"The lift is out," Hattie said, speaking to him for the first time since they had arrived at Child Services. She was out of breath following the three flights of steps they had just climbed. Appardly, too, was struggling for breath.

She led him along the hall to a room bearing a wooden sign-post which read "Oblong Dormitory". When he followed Hattie into the dormitory, he soon saw the reason behind the name — the room was an oblong shape.

There were half a dozen bunkbeds — capacity for twelve orphans, or runaways, or wherever these children had come from. There were three boys currently in the dormitory. Two of them had been lying on their backs on their lower bunks, dozing until Appardly and Hattie had come in. Now they propped themselves up on their elbows to get a better look. Appardly estimated them to be around twelve, thirteen years old. He couldn't help but notice the now-familiar sketching of the Huntharn Collective on the inside of their forearms. The third child in the room remained lying on an upper bunk on his side, his back to them, facing the wall. Much younger than the other two — six or seven, perhaps.

Appardly couldn't tell if this boy was similarly marked.

"Max?" Hattie said, addressing the child with his back turned towards them.

The child — Max — didn't react, continuing to face the wall.

Hattie shot Appardly a glance he found difficult to interpret. At first he thought it was one of those looks which said, *Do you see what I have to deal with?* but then he wondered if she wasn't just looking for some sign of sympathy — some degree of empathy — for the experiences these children had gone through ... were going through.

One of the boys on the bunks spoke up. "He won't say anything. He ain't got nothing to say." The boy who had spoken had clippered hair and the fluffy beginnings of a beard about his mouth and cheeks. "Hasn't said nothing since he got here. Not even to tell us his name. Max ain't his real name."

Hattie continued to focus on Max. "Would you like to go for a walk?"

Still no response.

She turned to the other boys. "Would you mind leaving us alone for a few minutes?"

The two boys remained where they were and then — with a shrug from one to the other — they slouched out of the room.

Hattie approached the bunk where Max lay. She breathed in gently, her shoulders dipping as if she was bracing herself for some great physical undertaking. Then she reached out and placed her palm flat on Max's shoulder. "Please. Please speak to us. This man here — hopefully he will be able to help you. The other boys too."

Max continued to face the wall. And then, as if there was a change in the very air itself, Max shifted, turning halfway to gaze at them.

He was identical to the one they had uncovered in the shipment.

Appardly gawped at the resemblance. And then he composed himself. "Do you remember where you came from?" Appardly asked. "It's important for us to establish that. Then we can find out how this all happened."

Outside the dormitory, there was a sound. Lowanna appeared in the doorway. How she had managed to navigate the house when the lift was non-operational escaped Appardly. But he knew better than to ask. She was trailed by the other woman from Child Services.

"We've just been to see another child — Adam — identical to the one we discovered."

"And this is Max," Appardly responded.

Lowanna's eyes widened and her lips parted slightly as she took in Max.

"We've been keeping them separated," Hattie said, picking up the conversation. "We didn't necessarily want them to be aware of one another."

When Appardly steered his attention back to Max, he was surprised to see that he was surveilling them all, taking in what was going on around him.

"Another one of me?" Max asked.

Hattie fluttered her eyelids. Appardly could tell she was unaccustomed to losing control. And that she had been taken off-guard by Lowanna's revelation that there were other boys just like him. "Yes, Max. Two others. That we know of so far."

"Why?" he asked.

"That's what we're trying to find out," Hattie replied. "Do you know anything?"

"I ... maybe," Max replied. "Did they say anything?"

There was a broad silence while the room absorbed the rare words from the boy's mouth. And then Lowanna responded. "No, they didn't say anything."

"Okay," Max replied.

"Do you have anything to tell us?" Lowanna asked.

Max's eyes widened. His lips parted slightly. "I ... I'm not sure. It's difficult to remember. The memories are all blurry. They don't make sense. I ... I feel as if someone is inside me. As if I have ... something ... something controlling me ... like a robot ..."

Appardly examined everyone else in the room, finally coming to rest on Lowanna. She was meeting his gaze. He knew that they were thinking exactly the same thing.

What had they stumbled upon?

An urgent notification appeared on Appardly's retinal display. He opened it:

Level 1 Emergency – Evacuate Immediately

———

Appardly stood stunned for several seconds. Of course he had his training. He knew exactly what he was supposed to do in his role as Customs House Manager. Only that he wasn't on the premises at that precise moment. When he attempted to contact Terri he was unable to establish a connection.

As he and Lowanna crossed the colony on a transport, information began to dribble in, scraps of reports appearing through colony media outlets.

There had been an explosion at the port. Although the source of the explosion was still not entirely clear, it followed that it would've been some spacecraft docked there. Hundreds of likely explanations flashed through his mind, although it was impossible not to return to the one which most closely tied into the matter they were investigating.

When Appardly and Lowanna arrived at the office, Colony Security had already established a perimeter. Before being turned away from the tape, he caught sight of several Interstellar Police officers prowling around.

And so this was being taken out of their hands now.

He thought of the children at Child Services. It wouldn't be long before IP paid them a visit. Now there had been bloodshed — or at the very least destruction of property — the stakes had been raised. Appardly wondered what might happen to those children, to Adam, Max and the unnamed third child. They would be taken away for questioning, of course.

But then what?

Soon after, Appardly established a connection with Terri who was able to confirm that none of the customs operatives had been injured by the blast. That they were all currently in the blast shelter, safe and sound. To those in the office, the explosion had been merely a severe earthquake. Appardly was surprised at how relieved he was to hear this news. He supposed that he wasn't as hardened by years of experience as he liked to believe.

"Doesn't this ever frustrate you?" Lowanna asked.

"Hmm?" Appardly replied.

"Never seeing these things through to the end?"

"What do you mean?"

"We'll never see those kids again. We'll never know where the mystery ends for sure. What that mark really meant."

Appardly continued to scan the area, taking in the constant toing and froing of various different types of emergency service. He was always in awe at the quality of their training — how they were like worker ants. Able to get on with their jobs no matter the circumstances.

Tapping into some hive mind.

Some higher purpose.

"Our job isn't to solve mysteries," Appardly said. "Our job is to shine a light on the evidence and then turn it over to the appropriate authority."

"What if we'd done nothing?"

"What do you mean?"

"If we hadn't followed up on the children. If we had just left them to Child Services. This was a warning — loud and clear. This" — Lowanna gestured to indicate the chaos and carnage before them — "is our direct fault. Don't you remember what Max was saying? That it was as if his body wasn't his own? As if someone was within him, working him like some sort of a robot? Doesn't it follow that this is the result?"

"Perhaps, perhaps not," Appardly replied. "If we had stood by and done nothing whatever is going on might've continued for years rather than coming to an abrupt head as it has done here. We've done a good job. Gone above and beyond."

Lowanna said nothing to this.

Appardly received another message through his Link. He scanned it quickly. Processing the message subconsciously. "Colony Chief Gomez is calling an emergency meeting."

"Do you think Gomez wants someone to take responsibility?"

"I think Gomez wants to know that everything is in control — and it is."

"But we haven't solved anything."

"So we'll tell her what we've found out."

Lowanna held her ground for another few seconds. He wondered if she was considering giving him her notice right there and then. He supposed he wouldn't have blamed her, thinking about her own position. If she wanted answers then this wasn't the right role for her.

She should join Colony Security.

But she eventually looked to him, waiting for him to take the lead.

As they boarded another transport, headed for the Colony Council Chambers, he looked away from the carnage. As they left it all behind, he couldn't prevent a wry smile breaking out across his lips. Splitting his mouth in two.

It was days like this that he relished his role. His office served its purpose.

It helped the colony stand strong.

RUPTURED SKY

Colony Chief Mangalden felt as if she was peeling apart at the seams. Her whole body convulsed with her sobbing. She was deeply ashamed to be seen in this way. She was ashamed that she had allowed herself to get into this state. Wasn't she supposed to be a grown-up woman? A woman in control of her own destiny?

A *career* woman?

Through the glass, she could make out the departing ship. She watched it hover above the spaceport pad — holding its place in mid-air for a long moment as if reserving a glower specifically for her — before shooting upwards at a frightening pace.

Making to break through the atmosphere.

To get away from Xenarth — the planet which she was trying her very best to make her home.

Often she dreamed of getting away from Xenarth herself. But that was inconceivable. In order for that to happen, she would need to give up her job here. She would have to admit failure. And she wasn't ready to do that now.

If ever.

That — quite frankly — had been the worst meeting of her life ... and that was putting it lightly. It had been a disaster from start to finish.

"Ma'am?"

Mangalden turned, only realising a second or two later that she was in no fit state to be seen by anyone. It was Grashens, her personal assistant. He was beanpole skinny and just as tall. Mangalden found herself worrying more often than was entirely healthy about whether a stiff breeze might do for him one day. Lucky for him there *was* no wind on Xenarth.

There wasn't much of *anything* on Xenarth.

Grashens met her eye. "I was just wondering if you would like me to cancel your four o'clock?"

Knowing she couldn't hide her appearance, Mangalden produced a tissue from the pocket of her overalls and dabbed at her makeup-smudged cheeks. "My four o'clock?"

"With Admiral Novu. About the extension to the access agreement?"

"Oh, yes ... No, don't cancel. We can't cancel. God, no. Was there anything else?"

Grashens eyed her closely. If she hadn't known better, she could've sworn that he was on the verge of breaking into tears himself. "No, ma'am. Meeting Room Four."

"Four at four. Fine."

Grashens left her.

Mangalden peered up into the heavens, watching the ship disappear into the dank black toxic fog which smothered the Xenarth sky. If it wasn't for the pressurised atmospheric Bubbles they inhabited it would've been impossible to live here.

She consulted her Link, toying with the idea of playing back footage from the meeting.

In the end, she resisted, though.

It served no purpose to dwell on past failures.

One should learn from mistakes, of course, but revelling in personal misery was about as helpful as punching yourself in the eye socket.

———

A tremendous burp tumbled out through the open door to Meeting Room Four and into the corridor. Mangalden wrinkled her nose as she trod her way towards the room. The last person she wanted to speak with right now was "Admiral" Novu.

Inside Meeting Room Four, Novu sat leaning back in her chair, her muddy boots resting on the polished table. She had a thermos containing some kind of liquor inches away from her soles. There was a transparent puddle where some of the drink had spilled.

Mangalden would've been sure it was liquor from the stench.

But she was made certain from Novu's expression.

"Viceroy!" Novu said, grinning inanely.

Mangalden shifted a glance about the room. She saw Novu wasn't alone ... not that she had expected her to be. She had brought along two large men. They wore baggy flight overalls designed to conceal seemingly any weapon of their choosing.

Novu herself, however, was scantily clad.

She wore a dirty-white crop top which exposed her tough muscular abdomen. Beneath, she had on a pair of tight-fitting black jeans. Although Mangalden hated to admit it, Novu made her feel somewhat dowdy in her plain work overalls. She was glad when Grashens arrived, in his work overalls too, unnecessarily apologising for his tardiness to everyone in the room.

"Your muscle?" Novu asked, taking a drink from the thermos, nodding to Grashens.

Mangalden said nothing.

Novu rocked her head back, her eyeballs becoming no more than squidgy white balls. She dropped her feet to the floor, propping her elbows on the table. She brought the thermos down with a slam, spilling more of the contents. "Chairman Douglas just blow out?"

Mangalden felt a tightness in her chest, like a swift slap across the cheek. She tried to compose herself but not before Novu had seen she'd gotten the reaction she was after. "Yes — I just had a meeting with him."

"That why you've been blubbing?"

Again Mangalden felt taken aback. She shifted in her seat, shooting Grashens a glance. He had turned a bright-red shade, his head bowed in faux concentration, taking notes.

"You wanted to see us about the extension?"

"Mm," Novu said, eyeing the thermos again, but this time apparently deciding better of having another sip. "We thought we might have an offer for you."

Mangalden looked again to Grashens. He was taking a record of the meeting using his Link. Like so many of those who seek to avoid confrontation, he seemed to roll into an ever-tighter ball — as if attempting to disappear into himself. Mangalden couldn't help noticing that one of Novu's men stared at Grashens without ceasing. She supposed this was all part and parcel of the intimidation tactics Novu had settled on before arriving at this meeting. That was the problem with dealing with outlaws — *gangsters* — it was all so theatrical.

Everything was a show of strength or a weakness exposed.

"Got you over a barrel, haven't we?" Novu said. "That why you went and got weepy over Dougie boy?"

Mangalden met her eye. She recalled the first time they had met. It had been in a bar downtown. They had been drawn to one another. They hadn't known one another at the time. They hadn't known how violently their paths would intersect in their day-to-day lives. How their nightly adventures would turn into scattered dreams, never to be repeated, once the truth was out. Mangalden hadn't known, in any case. The more she learned about Novu, the more she was convinced that every beat of her heart was a calculated façade.

"You know," Novu went on, "if I so wanted it, I could blow

Dougie from the sky. Think what that might do for your career aspirations, viceroy. I'd be doing you a favour. And then howabouts I do the same with the next one comes along. The next one. And the next. Till there's none of them left. Till *you're* the one that's in line. Then you'd be queen." Novu brought her thermos up to her lower lip. She pressed the rim into her skin, squeezing the blood away from the surface. "And what'd that make me, huh?"

"I have no idea."

Novu held her eye as she tipped the thermos up, drained it, and then tossed it over her shoulder. It clattered against the wall. "It'd mean I'd have me my own piece of the universe. Legitimate, like. My own personal princess angel pie."

Mangalden felt a firmness in her stomach. She breathed in deeply, to the bottom of her lungs, and felt her shoulders rise. "Look, if you've come to talk, then let's talk. I don't have time to waste, okay? I've got a colony to run."

"A 'colony', is that right?"

Mangalden said nothing.

Novu continued, "Let's not fool ourselves. A colony is all about people helping people. I'm talking the modern definition — not the historic. Now, this here's nothing more than a business operation. Okay, you got it, maybe it *is* a colony. One of them things from back on Earth in the nineteenth century. One of them places where you whip men, women and children to do your business. A *colony*. Your business is to keep these people down. For them to do what they're told. To get them to mine this planet empty."

"That's an awfully political sentiment for you."

Novu staggered forward, onto her feet. She was not tall so she had to stand to have any physical presence at all at the table. Her nostrils flared and her eyes flashed red. "You don't know nothing *about* me, lady. Listen, you think that because one or two times we got it on that you know me real deep down? That you got me all sussed out?"

Ordinarily Mangalden would've been appalled for something so personal to be paraded in a work setting, however today she was glad to get a rise out of Novu. She felt as if she was gaining some kind of leverage with the world again. "That's not what I'm saying," Mangalden replied. "What I'm trying to say is that we're both busy. We have things to attend to. Can we get to the point?"

Novu took a breath, pausing. Maybe it was the drink that was making her reactions so unpredictable — perhaps she *wanted* Mangalden to think it was the drink making her unpredictable. In any case, she collected herself now. " 'The point'. Okay, the *point* is that you've got a whole bunch of stuff down here, planetside, that you want up *there* in the sky. And we've got ourselves something of an impasse. Nothing goes up and stays up too long without my say-so now, does it?"

"No."

"From looking at the state of you — after that meeting with Dougie-boy — you need this to get sorted pretty bad. What's the deal? You down on profit? Need to recoup some cost? The payments you make to me to use *our* space too much for the Company? The last hike too much for the accountants? I'll bet you're pissing yourself to think I was going to ask for double what I'm already charging in this meeting. Admit it?"

There wasn't much point in denying it. Although Novu might be many things, she was especially perceptive. She had a gift for sniffing out just what had gone down. "That's about the measure of the situation," Mangalden replied.

"Well, then," Novu said, her tongue lolling onto her lower lip. "How'd Dougie speak to you? Pretty harsh from the looks of things. He tell you this was your last chance? That you needed to make nice with the space pirates? Get them to see things from your point of view?"

"You did say you had an offer for us."

This stopped Novu in her tracks. For a second, Mangalden was certain Novu was going to leap into a fresh outburst. That she was going to fly into a rage — perhaps jump up on the meeting room table and rush over to her. Maybe she'd even go so far as to lay a hand on Mangalden, just to show her that she could. The fact was that Colony Security were no match for the hundreds — *thousands?* — of ships Novu held at her beck and call.

Indeed, if she saw fit to do so, and she thought she might be able to outrun the IPs forever — Interstellar Police — then Novu might very well be tempted. As if she was determined to defy every one of Mangalden's internal predictions, Novu sat back in her chair and crossed her arms. "We want a piece."

"A piece of what?"

"Xenarth."

Mangalden's eyes near enough bobbed free of their sockets. "I'm sorry?"

"You heard me."

Mangalden shook her head, smiling. "I'm sorry, no. That's just not ... I don't have the authorisation to promise something like that. It's way above my head ... I ..."

"But you know who to talk to about it, don't you? You know who's got the *authorisation*. You can bring them around to your way of thinking."

Mangalden glanced over at Grashens. He was observing the exchange taking place. He made no effort to avert his gaze now. The two men Novu had brought with her were also at a higher level of alertness.

Mangalden breathed in deeply, trying to calm herself. She felt herself being swept back to the countless training courses she had attended on how to handle stressful situations. It was important to feel in control ... even when you weren't.

It was important not to bawl your eyes out, either.

"What do you want a piece of the planet for?"

"Does it matter?"

"I ... it might help my argument to my superiors."

"Reassurance?"

"Something like that."

"I want to go legitimate. I want a piece of land. Somewhere I can call my own. Sure, up there, I've got all the power I want, but it's nothing when you have no ... *firm* land to call your own. My power is a vacuum. I want something concrete."

"And what would you give us in exchange?"

"Full access — no conditions — and I'll even throw in a security agreement. That means that if any of your ships are fired on within this sector, one of my ships will be right there, ready —"

"We already have a security agreement."

"Not doing you much good, though, is it?"

"How long can you keep this deal on the table?"

Novu rose from her chair. She nodded to her escorts who also got up. "Till midnight tonight. After that it all goes away."

"Meaning?"

Novu trudged over to the doorway. "We're taking this planet whether you like it or not. It's just a case of how much blood is shed. How much you're willing to lose."

———

Mangalden sat on the edge of the marble fountain, at the centre of the Glory Gardens. She looked out across the colony, seeing the winking lights as the illumination dimmed into simulated night-time. It had just gone six thirty. Five and a half hours to go.

Mangalden liked to sit here after a hard day's work, which was more and more often these days. She liked the way she could switch her mind off ... how she could breathe in the gentle scent of roses, and freshly cut grass. How there was a dampness in the air — something which was sadly lacking in other areas of the colony.

Grashens sat beside her, though he said nothing. When Mangalden had invited him to come with her it hadn't been because she wanted the company. He was the only other person on the colony who had been present at that meeting with Novu just now, and she couldn't afford Novu's threat becoming common knowledge — through the gossip grapevine — until she had had a chance to think about how to deal with it.

Colony Chief Mangalden— or "Viceroy", as Novu preferred to mockingly refer to her — had the final say on most things that went on planetside. Something like this, though, giving over a portion of land to ... to *criminals* ... it was the kind of simplistic madness that went against all logic. And she knew she would make herself a fool with her superiors if she did as she had promised.

But if she didn't do as she had promised Novu would move in on the colony.

"Do you think she meant what she said?" Mangalden asked.

Grashens stared out ahead. "I ... wouldn't want to say for certain."

"Please, say something."

Grashens remained conflicted for a long moment. "It's difficult to say. With people like that. When they start making threats they're almost ... childlike. Overly emotional."

"So you think she may well mean it?"

Grashens attempted a smirk but the gravity of the situation appeared to strike him. No doubt the fact that they may well be facing an aerial assault that night had sunk in. "Thinking about it logically, it's ridiculous. There's no way she'd be able to take the planet. I mean, she might *take* it, but she wouldn't keep it long ... not once the IPs get a sniff."

"And do you think we'll be around when the IPs do show up?"

"Maybe we should be contacting them right now."

Mangalden allowed this to stew for a second or so. Even if she did get the ball rolling right away, she knew that they couldn't realistically receive the kind of support to repel Novu for about a week, or more. If she filed a call for help right at this instant, she might get lucky and draw a nearby patrol. But those patrols would be nothing compared to Novu's forces.

"Do you think it's all or nothing for her?" Mangalden asked.

Grashens shrugged. "I guess."

"What would you do in my place?"

"I would ... probably give her the piece of land." Grashens blinked rapidly, apparently checking himself. "After certain assurances, of course."

"Such as?"

"Well, there would need to be some strict boundaries put in place. An understanding that any criminal activity must be kept within their own agreed zone."

As Mangalden thought on Grashens's advice, she couldn't help but find herself swept back to the bar that night she had met Novu.

When neither of them had known anything about the other.

Mangalden had arrived on Xenarth no more than a week earlier. She had turned up planetside as an understudy for the outgoing Colony Chief. It had been a good time. Nobody had known her face then. Nobody would stop her in the street to tell her about their problems, and to tell her just how easily she could solve them ... It had been the most freeing experience she had had since leaving home. Since striking out on her own.

The lighting in the bar had been a flickering grey — perhaps it was supposed to have been silver. The music had been loud. The air had reeked of nondescript alcohol, and sweat. She had felt the damp heat squeezing into her pores.

And then she had seen Novu.

Sat at one of the barstools.

Feet dangling and kicking playfully like she was nine years old.

And then ... and then ... everything had happened so fast. And they had gone further than she could've imagined.

They couldn't have lasted more than two weeks — maybe three — when each of them realised who the other was.

One bad.

The other good.

Black.

And white.

The whole ridiculousness of the thing was that Mangalden couldn't even remember which bar they had met in. She supposed that if she really wanted to know, she could consult her Link. It would be able to retrace her movements back through her entire life.

But she preferred to use her personal, biological memories.

She found that using her Link to help her remember made her mind lazy.

In actual fact, she knew the truth was that she didn't want to rediscover the bar. She wanted to forget it existed.

In actual fact, this went beyond *wanting*, Mangalden was *compelled* to deny knowledge that anything had ever happened between her and Novu. Anything else and she knew she would be out on her ear. Especially now. Especially with her delicate current position.

"Well," Mangalden said, returning to the present, to Glory

Gardens and Grashens still sat patiently beside her. "I guess I can give peace and love a shot."

———

Mangalden's whole body shook as she pulled herself away from the wall. An artificial night-time breeze blew back her hair. It was nice, soothing, cooling. But it served only to stir up the embers in her belly. She had come up here — to the balcony of the Colony Chief's penthouse, her penthouse — to make the calls. She had hoped the surroundings would give her a calmer head. That she would be able to strike a reasonable tone of voice. It had been optimistic to expect she would get anything close to what she sought.

And optimism didn't go very far.

Not in business.

She used her Link to make the calls. The voices channelling directly into her inner ear — as clearly as if they had been standing right beside her.

The first person she had spoken to had been a sector representative at head office. Mangalden had made her case for the situation, referencing the meeting she had had earlier that evening with Douglas — Chief of Colony Hive F — with regards to a local issue they were having with criminal activity ... specifically in relation to the hijacking and destruction of cargo exiting Xenarth. The measures they had needed to resort to.

Negotiating with criminals.

This did indeed grab the sector representative's attention as he had not been sighted on the agreement which'd been struck — with Douglas's blessing — between the colony and the criminal element. Already, Mangalden felt her stomach sinking at the prospect of Douglas finding out about this act of insubordination. She began to obsess about how it might manifest itself. If he did find out, he wouldn't confront her with the matter, of course ... no, he would keep the information to himself and exploit the knowledge in subtle ways.

She waited patiently as the sector representative explained the Company's stance towards criminals, although in truth Mangalden could have recited the policy in her sleep.

Policies were all well and good inside an office building.

But things were different in the real world.

When she eventually floated the idea of offering the criminal element a piece of land in return for a permanent access agreement, coupled with a security agreement, the sector representative shut her down. Before she got kicked off the line, however, she did manage to get hold of the details of the Company president herself.

Or at least her personal assistant.

She had worked as hard as she could to get through to the PA. She had tried every last trick in the book to get put through to her boss. And in the end she had been successful.

Mangalden had thought she would feel a lot more tense about speaking directly to the president. She had never met her. But she had heard the stories. Everyone spoke about how stubborn she was so Mangalden was pleasantly surprised when the president heard her out on the whole issue, appearing to think the proposal through deeply before outlining to Mangalden in fewer than three bullet points exactly why they would never negotiate with criminals. Again, there was the insinuation that they were already on rocky ground from the temporary access deal they had already struck with Novu.

The Company did not negotiate with such elements.

She was quite clear on the fact.

It had been with an apologetic tone that the president had bid her good night.

As Mangalden surveyed the view of the colony from her balcony, it was the loneliest she had felt since she had arrived. Although she had always felt the distance from the rest of civilisation being out here, she had never felt truly alone until now.

It was her against some space pirates.

That was the truth of the matter.

And these people's lives were in her hands.

Hundreds of thousands of them.

It was past eleven o'clock now. The deadline was closing fast. She knew that Novu would be awaiting her call. Was Novu preparing her forces right away? Would she strike a few minutes after midnight?

Mangalden thought of contacting Grashens. Asking him out to her penthouse at this time of night. But she resisted. She really was clutching at straws now — just as she had been when she had plainly asked for his advice. What he might do in her shoes. She wondered what he must think of her now for even asking him that question.

Only one option remained.

———

It was far easier to get hold of Novu than the Company representatives. When Novu picked up the call, there was no tired tone to her voice. She seemed just as sharp as always. If she had been drinking then she didn't slur her words. "What can I do for you, Viceroy?"

Mangalden pressed her fingertips into her temples. She rested her elbows on the balcony rail and examined the drop below. Four, five storeys. If she took a tumble she wouldn't survive. "I'm getting nowhere," she said.

"Well, that doesn't sound too positive for your life expectancy. Or for the rest of those people down there."

"You're really going to do this?"

"If you don't strike us a deal."

"It's impossible. I've already made enough of a fool of myself. My ticket's been punched. I'm on borrowed time."

"Sorry to hear that, sugar lump."

Mangalden felt a tingle pass up her spine. That was the term of endearment Novu had used the first night they had met. And then the occasions afterwards. Novu had to realise it. Was this just another of her games? To bring Mangalden close, and then to walk away.

"You know, there is another way."

"What?" Mangalden replied, her voice feeling distant.

"Surrender."

" 'Surrender' ?"

"That's what I said. Have your boys stand down. Let us walk on in and take over. That's all. Plain and simple. We won't go after your operation. You can keep carrying on just as you have been. Just let us quietly go about our business. How about it?"

Mangalden wasn't quite sure how the tone had shifted in Novu's voice. There seemed to be a strand of desperation about it now. She took a shallow breath. She thought about what Grashens had said — about how there was no telling what someone like Novu would do. But at the bottom of everything hadn't Novu always been in control, deeply careful about what she projected about herself and her operation?

"I ... don't know," Mangalden responded. "I've had my answer. We're not to give up."

"Yeah, sugar lump, but I'm talking about you and me. I'm saying the two of us come to some agreement. This ain't about what corporate thinks best. Nobody needs to ever know."

"They'll find out in the end. One way or the other. Like I said, the questions I've been asking will draw attention. I doubt I'll be in this job much past next week."

"We can protect you — keep you here."

"What'd you mean?"

"Well, your people trust you. They listen to you. You have that much. Doesn't that count for something?"

"Not once they realise that the mining operation has been compromised. Not once the franchising cheques stop coming in and salaries start drying up."

"There are other places you can sell the payload."

Mangalden thought for a long moment. "I ... see what you're suggesting but it's ... not possible."

"Listen, what is and isn't possible is up for debate, sugar lump. Do you got that?"

"I thought you wanted to go legitimate. Something like this ... it would mean being on the run for the rest of your life. For the rest of *our* lives. What about the IPs? Aren't you worried they'll come for you? That they'll —"

"Fuck the IPs! We ain't gotta take orders from them like they're some kinda tsars. This's a big universe. Enough of a piece for everybody."

"If it's such a big universe then why don't you set up on your own planet? The life support equipment here belongs to the Company. You know that's their stake in this place. That and the natural assets we're mining. They won't let this slide. Think of all the time and resources they spent getting set up here. It's just common sense, Novu."

There was silence over the line.

"We can manage," Novu replied. "If I have your word that you'll stand by me, I'll promise that we can manage whatever threat comes out of those heavens."

Mangalden's heart beat hard against her ribs. It felt as if her blood was straining to burst from her veins. Her vision kept coming fuzzy. She felt her throat constricting. Memories were returning to her in a flood. She thought of her time with Novu — she had never laughed so much in all her life. All those memories she thought had been locked away forever. That was a dream, though.

"Listen up, sugar lump. Way I see it you can't lose. You take me up on this offer. You offer no resistance, well, that's gonna look like nothing but sense to the Company. Sure, they're bloodthirsty capitalists, but they're not idiots. They'll recognise that by surrendering to us you saved a lot of lives. If they do ever succeed in prying us off this rock then you'll be a hero. You'll be ..."

Mangalden somehow found the strength to speak up. "You think that if it comes down to it the Company really cares about all these lives? If it comes right down to it then they'll do anything to get their hands back on this planet. They'll shut down life support. Watch every last person choke to death down here. Then move in, clear away the bodies, and pick up where they left off."

"They ain't gonna manage that though, sugar lump, on account of what I already told you. We gonna keep them at a good arm's length. Better even. Why can't you trust me on this? What've you really got to lose?"

"My life. And the lives of all those on this planet."

"I can vouch for them."

"Can you?"

Novu's voice dropped to a husky whisper and Mangalden got the feeling — a feeling she had not experienced previously — that this was a level of sincerity that Novu did not commonly ascend to. "You know how many people in my life I given my word to — my *true* word."

"I'd hedge a few hundred thousand."

Novu gave a light chuckle. "Listen here, when I say all these things I'm not just saying them because they sound pretty. Because they sound like some kinda utopian vision sweeping through my dumb skull. It's because the fundamentals are already in place. Maybe I'm a bigger fish than you'd like to think. Or maybe I look stupider than I look. If we can work together on this then we can do something truly special. We can start something else entirely. Tell me that you've never thought of true frontiering? You know, homesteading?"

Mangalden felt a smile sneak onto her lips. Although she did her best to resist the joyful warmth rising in her gut, she knew that there was something about those words that held a power over her. She knew that it held a power over anyone who decided to leave one of the larger human settlements and go out into the further reaches of the universe in search of adventure. You had to be brave ... or, as Novu said, you needed to be stupider than you looked. Which one was Mangalden?

"I don't know what to say," Mangalden replied. "I mean, given the situation, the choice you are asking me to make, stepping aside to allow you to take over, or else having you wage mass murder against this planet, then I don't see that there *is* any choice."

"Now you're coming round to my way of thinking."

"But if the IPs do come sniffing around then we might just be pushing that whole mass murder thing back in time. If they do come, they'll be coming for all of us."

For the first time in what seemed like the whole time they had known one another, Novu spoke from the heart. "And I give you my word that we will protect you from them. From every other threat. That goes for the threat within, too, you understand? Although contrary to popular opinion, not every single one of my charges is a dyed-in-the-wool murdering, raping, pillaging delinquent. We just want our piece. Our time has rolled around."

Mangalden peered out across the colony another time. She thought of everyone down there — oblivious of what was taking place. Oblivious that their lives hung in the balance of the discussion she was having now.

It was mind-blowing that these people trusted her with their lives.

And she was determined not to let them down.

She spoke to Novu again. "So I just let you swan in, hands in the air — is that it?"

"I haven't thought through specifics. But, yeah, that's the general idea. You want some time to think it over?"

Mangalden glanced at the colony another time. She shook her head even though Novu couldn't see her. "No. What else can I say? You've backed me into a corner. There's only one way out."

"I knew you'd come round to my way of thinking, sugar lump. This'll be good. For both of us. I promise you that. Years later we'll look back on this. Think just why the hell we ever had any doubts at all."

When the line went dead, Mangalden looked long and hard at the drop from her penthouse balcony.

After about a minute, she drew herself back from the edge, went inside and made herself a drink. She felt a throbbing pressure at her temples. She was trembling all over.

This was the start of something, all right.

She just had no idea how it would end.

SCRIPTING MADNESS

E leana Redbank had hardly got herself free of the meeting
when she received the message from Gen on her retinal
display:

> *I'm sorry. It's not working. By the time you read this I'm*
> *gone. Good luck.*

"Good luck"? Eleana found herself mouthing the words in
disbelief. Just what in the hell was "good luck" supposed to mean?

She stopped walking. The clack of her heels ceased. She felt
the white polished tiling which covered the walls, floors and ceil-
ings blur into a puffy cloud.

Sorry.

Not working.

I'm gone.

Eleana resorted to the standard measure whenever she was
dealing with a tricky piece of script. When she was seemingly
unable to find a solution. She shut down her retinal display.
Unhooked herself from her Link.

She peered out of the window at the expansive cityscape
surrounding. She pictured herself as if she was in some film scene.
The camera sweeping out into a panoramic angle. And then she
thought of the superimposed text giving the location and time:

Armour Scripts. 1 3:3 1

Starring in a film was about the last thing she would ever want
to do.

Peering through the glass, she focused on a personal transport
weaving its way through the alleyway just below the building. She
thought of the scripts she and her colleagues at Armour had

written which governed the speed and direction of that transport. As a passenger alighted, she thought of the transaction being processed. That as the passenger had swiped their biometrics, the personal transport had corresponded with the city's transactional mainframe, which'd — in turn — contacted the passenger's bank, debiting the balance. The bank would communicate with the passenger's Link — send a courtesy notification that the transaction had cleared their account.

And then Eleana began to think of the bank itself.

The scripts in operation there.

All of the numberless customers.

Each of them going about their day.

Leaving their footprints in their transactional activity.

And then she caught herself. She knew that if she allowed it, her mind would get away from her. She would be unable to think of anything else all day.

Usually when dressed in her work outfit and standing at this window looking out over the city she felt as if she was a hundred-feet tall. Her work dress consisted of a well-cut jacket over a crisp white blouse. She liked how it made her look just a little manly although she always added a feminine touch. Today she had gone with a silver jacket and trousers with a pink feather poking out of the jacket pocket to give her some "womanly" softness. Then she'd made sure to use plenty of blusher to bring out the pink in her cheeks.

Gen always said she looked "plain", that she should take more risks. That instead of allowing her curly blond hair to fall in ringlets, she should get out some straighteners, allow it to flow down her back. That would be a start. Eleana herself had always had the urge to buzz the whole lot off.

All told, Eleana had been happy this morning.

She had had it together.

And now everything was falling apart.

Even though she was power-dressed and looking out over everything she helped operate, she felt as if she was shrinking. As if the city was growing up on all sides.

Pinning her in a personal jail cell.

Because Gen was gone.

They were up on the fiftieth floor here and she could see for miles and miles in the early afternoon light. Past the city boundaries. The clusters of trees which sprouted in suspicious little gangs on the fringes of the urban area. She had always fancied herself as being a country girl at heart. Just why she had ever believed that, considering that she had never spent anything more than a week or two out of the city, she really had no idea.

Sorry.

Not working.

I'm gone.

She brought her gaze back from the edges of the city. It was a beautiful day. Or it looked it. The sun beating down, a pleasant warmth rippling through the streets ... not that she'd know that here as the offices were air-conditioned to within an inch of their lives.

"Not jumping, are you?"

Eleana snapped back to reality. She took a second or so to blink away the confusion. She took in her colleague Karina standing beside her. She was wearing a tight black dress which showed off her milky white calves and accentuated all the delicate bones in her neck. Her hair — also black — was raked into a hair band. There was something effortlessly elegant about Karina. As Eleana knew from her own experience, it took a *ton* of effort to look *that* effortless.

"I know putting together summer-time adjustment protocols can drive a person to madness — but I wouldn't make a suicide out of it. That's a step too far." Karina leaned in closer so Eleana took a lungful of her minty perfume. "Your forehead's all furrowed. Your gaze is out of focus. Is your retinal display glitching?"

"No. I switched my Link off, actually."

"Then why're you looking so bugged out?"

"Just a migraine, that's all."

"A migraine about what?"

Eleana thought for a long moment. Too long as it turned out.

"Something romantic?"

"Hmm."

"Good romantic, or bad romantic?"

Although Eleana viewed Karina as the closest thing she had to a friend at work, there was still a distinction to be made between a "work friend" and a "friend friend".

Still, it didn't seem to matter.

Eleana's expression gave it all away.

"Bad, huh?" Karina replied, with a sigh. "Jesus, that stinks. Makes both of us." Karina sighed and then brought her arm up , pressing it against the glass. She placed her forehead against the back of her arm. "Shall we jump together?"

"We've got another meeting at three."

"True. We'd better be quick about it, then. Come on, I know the way to get up onto the roof so no one will know. We can make it if we try."

Despite herself — despite the shock Eleana still felt streaming through her blood at Gen's message — she felt herself smirk. "You'll have an HR case on us before you know it. People don't like to joke about that stuff. Not at work. Nobody's got a sense of humour."

"Yeah, well, who's around to hear it?"

"The walls have ears. Always."

Karina sighed long and hard, leaving a foggy imprint on the

glass. "Mm, no doubt some aural pattern-recognition routine. Something picking up on 'taboo subjects'. For all we know, they're using some code we helped write. We're tying the noose for our own necks." Karina examined Eleana, apparently searching for a reaction. When she saw she was getting none, she let out an exhalation of exasperation. "I hate all this ... *being professional*. Doesn't it suck you dry? Don't you ever want to just cut free and go do your thing elsewhere?"

"What 'thing' ?"

Karina drew back from the window, allowing her arm to drop down by her side. "Oh, you know, any*thing* that you want to do. On your own terms."

"You mean get rich and not have to work."

Karina brightened. "Yeah — that sounds promising!" Karina stepped away from the window and Eleana. "Well, if we're not jumping then I guess I'd better go make a start on prepping. Don't want to get caught without a plan."

As Karina left her behind, Eleana couldn't help but feel a sad little emptiness. She knew when she got back home that night there would be no one waiting for her.

Gen's bags would be gone.

There would be no trace of her ... or maybe it would be worse than that. In the weeks to come, she might uncover a stray sock here, some kerchief or trinket there. Cruel reminders of what they had had. Of what *she* had had.

But — like all her relationships in the past — she had blown it.

And right when she had believed this was a fresh start. She had landed this job six months ago. Things had looked good. But now everything had turned to shit.

Again.

———

A dizzy spell struck Eleana minutes into the meeting. It was with a private client wanting to cobble together some code that would help them monitor a series of droids she had tending a solar harvesting operation. The initial provider had done most of the work on the tech and the software backend, but had pulled out — *gone silent* — when the client had attempted to get in touch about droids bugging out. Although this was something Eleana normally found fascinating — she always loved getting her hands on some crappy code, fixing the problems, making it work like it should — she found it impossible to focus.

As if someone had struck her temple with a rubber mallet.

She wondered if she might not be developing a cold.

That morning on the MagRail someone had sneezed right on top of her. She had been expecting to cultivate a sickness of some sort. That always happened to her in times of stress ... times like these. She would consult her Link after the meeting to check to see if there was any change in her vital signs. Various different levels of code would speak to one another and she would be recommended a prescription and given a course of instructions on the optimal way to recover. There was a program she had worked on several months back which she had been impressed with. Secretly she had been waiting for herself or Gen to get sick so she could try it out.

Words continued to burble past her. The screen filled with scripts — lines and lines of code — snaking in through one side of her skull and right out the other. It was impossible to make sense of the whole. She was thoroughly distracted, like some wayward teenage student, constantly looking out the window.

At the world outside.

In a rare lucid moment, she returned to the room. Saw that Karina was staring at her across the table. For a long few seconds, Eleana found herself staring into her hazelnut eyes, losing herself.

Thinking of the possibilities. Could it be that what she had been searching for had been right in front of her all these months? That it would be something so pedestrian, so mundane, as a work colleague?

The only thing they had in common was work.

And — it seemed — bad luck in romance.

As the meeting came to an end, Eleana prepared herself for the evening ahead. She decided that she would work late. Take dinner in the office. She had rationalised this to herself in multiple ways. Firstly, it would mean that any chance of her bumping into Gen returning to the house to pick up something she had left behind would be mitigated. And, secondly, working late would mean that by the time Eleana eventually did get home, she wouldn't have energy to do anything but collapse into bed. And think of nothing. She had a ton of things to be getting on with, in any case. Chief among them, she needed to go back over the meeting earlier. She needed to know where to get started on the project.

When Eleana returned to her work station, she fell into a daze, flipping through her scripting library, examining the programs she had been working on throughout the day. She pored over the code, tagging what needed to be looked at a second time, things that she hadn't got quite right. Trying to take note of problems before they appeared.

The clock had slipped past six o'clock in the evening — an hour past her contracted work time. She thought of how somewhere a program was taking note of this. How the time she was working was now being added to her accrued leave account — time for her to claim at a later date. As Eleana bowed her head to examine the code for one of the droids which'd gone haywire on the solar harvesting facility, she sensed someone leaning over her.

When she looked up, she saw Karina, her hair now loose, hanging down like silk.

Eleana wanted to stroke that hair. She wanted to feel it up against her skin. It made her think of Gen's long hair. How she could run her fingers through it for hours — not saying anything. Just feeling its softness.

"You wanna get a drink?" As earlier, a minty scent clung to Karina. It made Eleana feel somehow more alert. More in the moment. More *awake*. "Something to eat, maybe?"

Still feeling stunned, Eleana glanced at the code she was confronted with and then examined the last few messages in her inbox. It could wait for tomorrow. Everything could wait for tomorrow. Everybody else had gone home. "Um, okay."

When Eleana rose, she realised that the rest of the office was empty. That the cleaning droids had already started on their evening rounds. This wasn't the first time this had happened. Whenever she got into her work — and especially when she submerged herself in scripting — she lost track of what was going on around her.

———

Outside, Eleana found that having Karina with her gave her something to focus on.

Streetlamps were just starting to blink on in the early-evening light. Eleana studied the backs of Karina's legs, feeling as if they were guiding her to some prearranged destination. As if this was a scene from some kind of prophetic painting. As if Eleana herself was nothing more than one of those droids or drones she programmed day in, day out … following protocols and orders as decided by their human masters.

Karina had a place in mind. Although Eleana had lived in the city for almost the whole of her life, she had resisted exploration as far as she was able.

She had always been afraid.

There was something innately scary about setting foot out of the front door. An air of unpredictability about the real world. That was what she liked about writing scripts. Whenever something went wrong, the way to solve it was always logical ... no matter how long it might take to unravel. Just like those droids who were no longer performing their tasks reliably on the solar harvesting facility. She could only imagine the chaos at present. The droids neglecting their tasks. Humans, as Eleana had learned again and again as she had worked scripts, were always inclined to focus far too much on individual details. She knew that the client was seeing the bounty decrease. That the solar panels were gathering a lower level of energy than previously. This would in turn affect revenue which would in turn affect the viability of the business as a going concern. However, it was overly simplistic to assign events to a simple linear sequence. Eleana knew she had to examine everything she could see on the surface and then dive deeper than the client could appreciate in order to reach the crux of the problem. That was how she earned her corn.

The bar was called El Tesoro. From outside, it looked dim, and inside it was even darker. There were orange lamps arranged on battered and beaten mahogany tables. Customers sat tending to their drinks. Most customers were either in couples or drinking on their own. It wasn't the kind of place for a big group — the wallpaper on the walls soaked up sound, deadening the buzz of conversation big groups cultivated. Eleana viewed this as a good thing since she was not into the types of places where "big groups" liked to go.

Karina selected a table off to one side of the bar and then

promptly shrugged her jacket into the chair. "What're you having?"

"I ... whatever you're having."

Karina rolled her eyes. "Typical submissive response. You really do want to be my bitch, don't you?"

Eleana was taken aback by the frankness of Karina's tone. But, then again, what had she expected? She was the one who had accepted the invitation ... she was hardly a naïve schoolgirl. There had been some flirtation. Just what had she expected to happen?

What did she *want* to happen?

Was she thinking clearly?

Of course she wasn't. Whenever her focus let up, her idle thoughts drifted onto Gen. And then she felt her heart swelling in her throat. Her whole body beginning to wilt.

As Eleana sat at the table, Karina ordered at the bar, returning with a pair of White Russians. "So," Karina said, "what's got you so sad?"

Eleana decided there was little point of trying to be coy now. She had got herself into this situation. And both she and Karina knew why they were here. She sipped her drink. "My girlfriend left me."

"That so," Karina replied, eyeing her over the rim of her own glass.

A silence filled in the gap between them.

Then Karina spoke up again.

"How long were you together?"

"Six, seven months."

"Well, which is it? Six or seven?"

"I think it was seven."

Karina spread her fingers around her glass. "Well, there, you see? That's your problem. You've got to be more committed than that. You've got to know these things. What was her name? Was she a fox?"

"I ... well." Eleana subconsciously opened up her inbox on her retinal scanner and flipped through her latest messages. There was nothing from Gen. She often checked her messages when she found herself in an uncomfortable situation. Her Link provided her with some kind of shield — allowing her to focus inwardly. To block out the world around her for a few choice moments. "Her name was Gen ... Genalt ... yes, she was attractive."

"Really?"

Eleana looked past her inbox at Karina. "Yes, I think so."

"And what sorts of things did you like to do together?"

"Oh, you know, just the usual things. Everyday things. Eating together. Going for walks. Taking holidays ... we were just settling in. It all seemed —"

"Sudden?" Karina had almost finished her drink now while Eleana was still only three or four sips into hers. "What did she do?"

"She was a painter."

"Make any money?"

"No, yes ... not enough."

"She work in a bar — place like this?"

"Uh, in a café ... for a while, anyway. But I was ..."

"Helping her out?"

"A little, yes."

"Typical. How old was she? Younger?"

"No, about the same age."

Eleana glanced about. She wanted to find some way out of this conversation. She knew it had been a mistake to come here. She would've been better off going back home. She might've been lonely — she might've bumped into Gen leaving ... but it would've been better than this interrogation.

Karina's lips split with a smile. "Sorry. I'm asking a lot of questions, aren't I? I'm being nosey. Getting in your business. It's just interesting, you know. How we all work together and yet we know so little about each other's lives."

Eleana had to admit that she didn't find it all that interesting. In fact, she was willing to go as far as to say that it was normal.

"Go on," Karina said. "Ask me some questions. See what I say."

"I ... don't know what to ask."

"Anything you like."

Eleana felt herself floundering. It wasn't in her nature to be assertive. To ask awkward questions. But this time she found one tumbling out. "Why're you interested in me?"

Karina's smile widened. Her cheeks went a little rosier. "Why *wouldn't* I be interested in you?"

"I don't know — I think I'm boring."

"You can't say that. You're the worst judge of your own character."

Eleana felt Karina's hand make contact with her knee below the table. It sent a ticklish electrical shock through her thigh. She squirmed in her seat. "I just don't think there's anything to interest you."

"Attraction doesn't always make sense, though, does it?"

"I ... suppose not."

They sat like that, with Karina gripping Eleana's leg for several more moments before Karina relinquished her hold. She arched her back and then shook her foamy, empty glass. "Another?"

Eleana saw that her own glass was still half full. But then she thought of returning to her flat. The emptiness there. The *loneliness*. And her will broke. "All right."

It was around midnight when Eleana finally succumbed to a yawn. After the second drink, the world had become much fuzzier. A great deal warmer. And she had found herself growing to cherish Karina's company all the more.

She had started to feel herself *growing into* her company.

When a couple had vacated a cushioned bench in the corner of the bar and gone home, Karina and Eleana had moved away from their table to take up their place there. Karina sat close, and Eleana savoured her warmth. She had to admit that she had also savoured Karina's delicate fingers spread upon her thigh. It was only now, as Karina had gone to visit the ladies and Eleana was alone again, that she realised how much she craved physical human contact.

And then she thought of Gen.

Her whole face became warm.

And her body felt stiff.

What was she doing here?

Why was she here?

Eleana switched her attention to her Link. She looked to her retinal display. Examining her inbox. There were no messages from Gen. She supposed she might've expected something. Some explanation. Why hadn't she sent a message back? ... Was it because she had sensed a certain cooling of their feelings to one another. Now that Eleana thought of it, countless episodes entered her mind. There was her work, of course. Eleana was so often busy that she would miss out on spending time with Gen. And then there was the fact that they didn't understand one another. Not really. They didn't understand what was important to each of them. They didn't understand the jobs each of them did ... Eleana could recall all of those nights when she had attempted to explain the importance of what she did at a detailed level, only to see Gen's eyes glazing over.

Eleana supposed the same happened whenever Gen started to talk about her art.

It wasn't that Eleana wasn't interested — she thought Gen's interests worthwhile — it was just that she couldn't see how she would ever manage to make it work. Eleana had already carved out a neat career path for herself. She knew where she would be in five years' time ... which position she would like to occupy within Armour — or another scripting company ... Gen, though, was far more nebulous.

There was no clear goal. No milestones to measure a path.

It was something Eleana believed she would never understand.

Karina returned from the ladies. Even though Eleana was aware that she was somewhat tipsy herself, she could tell that Karina had had more to drink. Karina was having trouble walking in a straight line, needing to seek the assistance of nearby tables and chairs to offer her stability. When she returned to the table, she stopped, standing several strides away, appraising Eleana where she continued to sit on the bench. Karina closed one eye as if analysing her. "You're still thinking of her ... aren't you?"

Eleana met Karina's gaze. She felt soppy, and warm from the drink. "Yeah."

"This will help — I promise." Karina clenched a half-finished glass in her fist and threw the contents at her.

Eleana saw everything happen in slow motion. She tried to evade the liquid flopping through the air but it was too late. Most of the liquid caught her in the face, with the rest soaking her work blouse. It was cold and ... well, wet.

An aftershock ripped through Eleana. A haze descended. She saw Karina — the stupid grin on her face, the now-empty glass she held down at her side. She breathed in the warm smell of coffee and cream, tinged by the medicinal, vapourlike smell of vodka.

The White Russian which had soaked her.

Karina appeared to recognise the seriousness of what she had done the second after she had taken stock of Eleana's expression. Her hand moved to cover her mouth. "Oh, I'm sorry, will you forgive me? ... I didn't mean ..."

But before Karina got the chance to finish, Eleana turned on her heel and bolted from the bar. She bowed her head as she retreated, cursing herself under her breath, the warmth brought on by the alcohol now lost — any feeling of companionship Karina had offered completely evaporated.

This had been a mistake.

A *big* mistake.

What had got into her?

———

At the office the next day, Eleana picked out an emerald dress from deep within her wardrobe. For a second, she convinced herself that it was Gen's. It had taken her many moments' thought to recall the day she had purchased it. Before she had met Gen. About a week before. She had never worn it — she hardly wore dresses at all.

But she would wear it today.

When she had returned to the flat the previous evening and flipped on the lights, the sight had put her in mind of those films set in prison camps, when the floodlights would send the shadows scurrying for the corners. Eleana had felt like an alien prying through her own personal space. Seeing to all of the places where Gen had kept her things. All her clothes were gone. The easel in the spare room was no longer there. And neither were the oil paints, or the canvases resting up against the wall. The only reminder was the odd mark here or there on the walls.

Reminders of the objects which'd once been there.

The person who had once lived here.

Until she had made a mess of everything.

Again.

Before she went to work, she made a trip to the hairdresser, getting a trim. It always made her feel sharper to know that her loose and frayed ends had been taken care of ... that everything linked up in a neat line.

As she sat in the chair at the hair salon, she flipped through her inbox, checking to see if there was anything from Gen. She wasn't in luck. Perhaps it was the sleep deprivation — maybe she was still in shock — but she found herself composing a message to Gen.

She wanted to see that she was all right, if nothing else.

At least that was what Eleana told herself on the surface.

In reality, she knew she cherished the hope that Gen would return. That there had been some misunderstanding. That they still had a future together.

This hope was soon banished by the automated response — reporting that the sender had blocked all messages from her. That was that, then.

As Eleana clacked her way to her desk at Armour Scripts, she noticed heads moving away from their business to stare at her. For a few seconds, they probably thought she was a new arrival. That they hadn't seen her before.

Every day.

It was miraculous what an emerald dress and a haircut could do for a girl.

Right away, Eleana sought out Karina. They had several meetings together today and they only worked a few desks apart so it was hardly likely that they would be able to avoid one another. She had decided that she needed to clear the air. That she needed to apologise for her behaviour. Karina had been drunk

— they had *both* been drunk — and it had been Karina's intention to make her feel better. She had just been wanting to cheer her up.

She had just gone about it the wrong way.

Karina was already at her desk, apparently absorbed in her work.

"Morning," Eleana said.

Karina gave her a sleepy smile. "Guess you had a chance to scrub up, huh? I don't think I can remember another time when I've seen you in a dress, and I like to think that I've been paying attention. The hair too. It suits you. Brings out the curve of your jawline."

"I wanted to look different."

"Different is good." Karina glanced about as if their boss might be making her way towards them. As if their boss might be able to rumble their conversation. There was nobody nearby — nobody even in earshot — but Karina leaned into her all the same. "I'm sorry about how I acted last night. I was childish. I said I wanted to help you ... but, the truth is that I wanted to be with someone. I'm so goddamn tired of being lonely. I got carried away. Something snapped in my brain. What I did was stupid. Do you forgive me?" She reached out and gently laid her fragile fingers on Eleana's forearm.

Eleana felt a warm thrill pass across the surface of her skin. Her heart beat faster. "And when something goes 'snap' in your brain does it always entail tossing a White Russian in someone's face?"

Karina shrugged and allowed her fingers to fall away from Eleana's skin. "It doesn't need to be specific. Whatever blunt object is closest to hand will usually do." She twisted her smirk into an earnest smile. "Did I really blow it last night?"

Eleana felt her blood thawing. And then she sighed. "Listen, it was my fault too. I've got a lot on my mind. It's ... difficult. Everything has happened so quickly. I'll need some time."

"Okay," Karina said. "That's fine — I'll give you all the time you need. Don't worry. When you're ready we'll talk."

All of a sudden, Eleana's face felt hot. She was close to tears. She knew that she should beat it for the nearest women's toilets. Lock herself in a cubicle for fifteen minutes and allow her tears to run their course. She still hadn't had time to properly grieve Gen's loss, after all. However, as Eleana plotted her disentanglement from Karina, she heard a familiar voice.

"Eleana?"

She turned to look. The warming sensation in Eleana's blood shrivelled into a biting chill. It was Gen.

To begin with, Eleana found herself passing her eyes across her entire surface area. Taking in her whole body as if this was a phantom which had appeared before her eyes: the sleek, trimmed frame, womanly curves at hips and chest. How her uncombed dark hair hung down to her shoulders. Her sweet, voluptuous lips. She was wearing a pair of beige overalls over a black-and-white striped top. She looked so out of place here among the desks. "I ... can we talk?"

Eleana froze. She knew everybody in the office was staring. And then she returned to reality. Her mind switched back onto its pragmatic rails. She picked her way across the office, doing her best to press on a professional smile. She ignored the eyes tracing each and every one of her movements, guiding Gen into one of the meeting rooms to the side of the main office. Once they had sat down in the small room — soundproofed but with windows out to the office and to the cityscape outside — Eleana finally allowed herself to breathe.

"Hi," Eleana said, unable to keep herself from smiling. Somehow she had come to the belief that she would never see Gen again. And she had never bargained for just how pleased it would make her to see Gen's face. "Where're you staying?"

"With friends."

Eleana nodded in response, bowing her head. She knew that everyone in the office was still watching. But they wouldn't be able to hear her words. That was something. "I ... I didn't see this coming. I'm sorry things got this bad. That ... they've turned out the way they have." She glanced up, taken off-guard to see tears glittering in Gen's eyes.

Somehow she had expected Gen to be immune to emotion from their split — as if because she was the one who had taken the decision she had no right to feel aggrieved.

"It's fine. When you make your mind up then that's the end, I suppose."

Eleana's thoughts stopped dead. She knew she had a bad habit of reading things too literally. Of seeing binary truths when there was far more depth to be had. She knew she was just as guilty of short-sightedness in the real world as her clients were when it came to the technology functioning in their enterprises. And yet, she was certain something was wrong.

"I ... thought you were the one who made her mind up?" Eleana said. "When I tried to send you a message this morning, the service told me you had blocked me. That's why I'm surprised to see you here. I didn't think you would ever want to see me again."

Gen stared at her for a long while and Eleana breathed in her familiar, creamy, grassy scent. Just the smell of her made her nostalgic — made her want to return to how things had been. "You were the one who told me to get out."

Silence fell upon them.

"I think something's going on here," Eleana said. "Can you send me the message you received from me?"

Gen glared. "Why? Are you going to deny sending it?"

"I can send you the message you sent me."

"I didn't *send* you a message."

They stewed in silence another few moments. And then, with seemingly no motion from Gen, Eleana received a forwarded message from her. Sure enough, it was tagged as having been sent by Eleana yesterday. Holding up her end of the deal, Eleana forwarded the message she had supposedly been sent by Gen.

The two of them read their messages in silence.

Eleana looked hers over:

It's time to move on, don't you think? We are so different. Our lives don't connect. We don't speak to one another. Not really. It's time for us to move apart, alone. That's the only way we can progress. I can help you find somewhere to stay but it's time for you to go. I'm sorry.

Eleana snapped her neck up, fixing on Gen. "I never sent this. This isn't my message."

Gen's eyes widened, also in disbelief. "This isn't mine, either. Then how ... someone else must have sent these. Someone else got access. They ..."

Eleana exchanged glances with Gen, and then felt her following her gaze as she peered out through the window to the office space, instinctively settling upon Karina's desk.

It was empty.

————

Eleana requested the rest of the day off work, rearranging the meetings she had scheduled. The two of them went into a café just along the street from Armour Scripts. Steam rose into the air, milky and hot. The windows were steamed up and there was the buzz of conversation. As confidential of a milieu as they were likely to find.

She told Gen what had occurred the previous night. That she had gone for a drink with Karina in a nearby bar ... that Karina had acted in an oddly flirtatious manner with her throughout the day. Although Eleana did her best to leave out the part where she had responded, she knew that Gen caught on.

Eleana spoke her thoughts aloud. "She has the skills, she could've gained access, she had the know-how. If she'd wanted to send those messages she could've done so."

"We need to contact the police."

Eleana waited a beat. "Yes, we do."

"What she did wasn't only illegal ... it was madness. Borderline psychotic."

Another uneasy quietness fell over them.

Everything had clicked into place so quickly. The events of the past twenty-four hours had left Eleana dizzy. She was still trying to catch up. As Eleana thought on the matter more and more, she couldn't help but see desperation behind what Karina had done.

Of course, there was flattery, too.

Karina had decided to hack into both Eleana and Gen's Links to manufacture a breakup between them so that she might claim Eleana for herself. It blew Eleana's mind that she could've felt so strongly towards her. And then she thought about what Karina had said about them hardly knowing anything about one another.

She supposed that — at least from Karina's end — that was not entirely true.

"It's funny," Gen said, head bowed, tracing the rim of her empty cup of coffee with her fine index finger, "you know, that message, even knowing that it wasn't from you, it rakes things up. I mean, I should've *known* it wasn't from you. It's the kind of thing that you would never write. Oh, the practicalities were there. The logical steps taken to the logical conclusion. It was an imitation of how you might think ... from the point of view of a fantasist. And yet, there was some truth there." She glanced up. "Don't you think?"

"What, that we're different?"

"Yeah."

"Well, that much is obvious, isn't it?"

"Do you think it'll ever work?"

Eleana stared back into Gen's eyes. She loved the girlish simplicity to her. The simple questions she asked which had complex answers. Her heart bounced up to her throat. She reached across the table for Gen's hand. Her skin was cool, rubbery. "I want to make it work — I can't imagine not having you in my life. I ... don't know what I would do ..."

"But we're so *different*. We see things so *differently*. And now this. It's all about control, isn't it? Everything you do? Moving pieces about a board. Having everything under your command. Making *sense* of everything." Gen moved her hand out from beneath Eleana's, propping her head up with her palm instead. "How do I know you're not going to hack into my head one day? How do I know you haven't hacked into my head already?"

Eleana peered out into the street, thinking she might see Karina passing by, making a sly escape. But there was no sign of her. Would Eleana be able to continue working here? It would be difficult to carry on. Although she liked to think she was above gossip and back-chatter the truth of the matter was it would affect her one way or another.

She turned back to Gen. "You have to trust me, I suppose."

"Hmm, yeah. I suppose I do."

"Just as I have to trust you."

Gen smirked and then rolled her eyes. "There's only so much damage that paint down a canvas will do."

They passed the rest of the afternoon in the café — not saying much to one another.

Going over old ground.

Making vague promises.

Never really seeing eye to eye.

When they left, Eleana was certain to look carefully around. There was no sign of Karina. But had she expected to see her there? Had she *wanted* to see her there?

She couldn't say for certain.

The only thing she could say with certainty was that she would never see her again.

HABITAT

"Do you know what your problem is? You're just so goddamn vain!"

Patric Zeethmeister's wife Evelyn stood before him, hands on her wide hips, her long blond hair turned frizzy by the Amazonian humidity and hanging down in clumps beneath the climbing helmet she wore. Dark patches of perspiration covered her tight-fitting quick-dry outfit which showed off her large breasts more than she would have liked, Patric was sure. Her complexion had turned a deep red colour from exertion and the rising mid-morning heat.

The two of them stood on a canopy viewing platform which was a fancy way to describe some nailed-together planks of wood sitting on the branch of the kapok tree they had just climbed. They were thirty, forty foot up in the air and could see for miles and miles, the thick foliage of the surrounding area against the blazing blue skies. In order to get here, they had shimmied their way up a rope using a mechanical ascender their guide had prepared for them. The task had been more manual labour than Patric liked to indulge in on a regular basis, not to mention on holiday. Over the side of the platform, Patric could see the guide making his way steadily up the rope to meet them. He obviously had much more practice than they did at this — a much better physical condition than two chunky tourists — and so he was ascending three times as fast.

Patric shifted his cool focus away from his wife and onto the calming sounds of the Amazonian rainforest all around them. Although he had no access to his neural Link here — he was unable to connect to any network and find out for sure — he thought the temperature must be well into the high twenties. He breathed in the thick, moist air, feeling the one-hundred percent humidity making every hair on his body tingle. He could hear howler monkeys nearby. With his tongue, he worked to free a morsel at the back of his teeth from the patarashca their guide had prepared for their lunch. It'd been too oniony for his taste, over-seasoned with coriander and fish would never be his favourite, but out here he had to take what he was given. This wasn't his habitat. He knew nothing about lighting fires, or the laws of nature. He was a native of cities — an expert in the human condition.

Or so said his professional success.

Patric switched back to his wife. He imagined his appearance was less than perfect right now. His black hair he liked to keep combed back and in place neatly atop his head would be frayed and wild beneath his own helmet. His slight paunch was peeping out over his too-tight, elasticated quick-dry trousers. Was it possible to be vain when he was as self-aware as he was? It was his *job* to be self-aware. And not only that, but self-aware on behalf of others. "I was just making a suggestion — that's all. If I can see a way of improving something then I come right out and say it. You know that about me. You've *always* known that about me."

"You *upset* him," Evelyn replied, pointing at the ascending guide. "There was no need to humiliate him."

"I didn't humiliate him. He just took it badly. They're not used to criticism out here. They're close-minded. They can't see beyond the 'ways of the jungle'. I've seen their smug little knowing grins, how they think they're better than us. How they think we're the crazy ones."

"Shut up — he's almost here."

"The guy barely speaks English. He probably didn't under-stand a word I said. Probably wouldn't even understand a word we're saying now."

Evelyn glared at him.

The steady zipping sound of metal on rope got louder as the guide propelled his way towards them. Patric took a moment to assess his appearance. He had no access to his Link here but when he worked with clients he would often take covert footage of them in action, to try and get them to see how they appeared to the world. It surprised him how far off people were when they thought of how the world perceived them. Once he had shattered the illusion of how they *thought* they appeared to the world, he would go about showing them how to change it. How to project the image they wanted. Allow them to achieve their aims. That was the foundation on which he had grown the business which had paid for countless holidays such as this one to the Amazon.

Life Motivator, Inc.

The guide powered up the final dozen or so tugs, dragging himself up the rope and onto the platform. His sleeveless vest clung tightly to his muscular chest. Like them, he was covered in perspiration, although Patric was certain the guide would never have acknowledged it. No, this was an Unshakable Man of the Jungle. Perfectly adapted to his environment. Not just another piece of sweaty man meat stumbling about.

Crouching down, the guide flipped a glance at the two of them as he reeled in the climbing rope, coiling it into a pile. Patric saw the unmistakable hurt in his expression. Although it pained him to admit it to himself, he could see Evelyn was right. He had hurt the guide's feelings. There was only one thing to do.

He would put her right for calling him vain.

"Listen," Patric said. "I'm sorry if what I said offended you. I was just offering a different worldview. I wanted to see if you had considered all sides. What I meant to say when I asked you if you'd ever had a 'real' job was whether you'd ever worked in an office. And when I asked if you'd ever consider moving back to be 'amongst the living', I meant to ask whether or not you would ever like to move to a city, you know, where there are more things going on." He caught Evelyn's eye, seeing her giving him a scowl and he knew this wasn't the apology she had had in mind. That was the thing about women, they always wanted everything to be comprehensive, done properly, and while that was totally fine with him, it was also sometimes impractical. There wasn't always time to blow through some step-by-step analysis of how everyone's emotions had been put out of place.

He tried again.

"You see, it's my work. It's difficult for me to switch off. I have to be critical all day. It's nothing to do with you." Again he caught a glare off Evelyn, and he immediately knew this wasn't going well. If only she could see how smoothly and expertly he manipulated people throughout his day job then perhaps she wouldn't think to criticise him so readily. It wasn't like he ever took her to task on her own specialty, although — granted — the amount he knew about pharmaceuticals would not fill the back of a modest-sized matchbox.

As Patric studied the side of the guide's face, he wasn't sure whether or not he was making himself understood. Or if he was only making things worse. But if the man had understood enough to be offended by what he had said then surely he understood what he was saying now.

If only he had access to the Link he could've booted up a translation program — he could've spoken to the man directly in his own language. And then — with a slightly wry internal grin — he thought that if the man had been fitted with his own neural device he might've been able to speak to him and his wife in flawless English.

That would turn the tables.

"We go across now," the guide replied, indicating the rope bridge which was connected to the platform on which they stood.

It hung across the canopy, the other end attached to another platform, about a hundred yards away.

———

That evening at dinner, Patric felt restless. Although the guides had warned him about venturing too far from camp, he ignored this particular advice and took the five-minute walk down to the river bank. Across the river, the sun was setting, placing the clouds opposite him in a reddish haze. He could hear crickets, or whatever their exotic cousins sounded like. There was the odd thrash out in the water which he put down to some fatal encounter between predator and prey. Although he had really done his best not to think about it — to not *try* — he again attempted to gain a connection to the Link. He knew that it was a matter of compulsion; that he was responding to some sort of a chemical imbalance in his brain, and yet he was unable to help himself. He thought of all the messages he was missing out on by being here, in the middle of nowhere, all of those problems he would need to return to following this trip and take care of ... he might as well get a little peek right now; that way he could get ahead, even just a little ...

As it became darker, he decided that he should head back to camp. He smelled cooked fish on the air and knew that dinner would soon be served. There was the gentle buzz of chatter, too, as the diners all emerged from their lodgings.

The camp itself was a collection of wooden cabins, all interconnected by a series of raised log walkways. Everything was a few feet off the ground. He supposed this was a provision for the rainy season when land would tend to flood around here. When he and Evelyn had arrived here yesterday afternoon, he had been pleasantly surprised by the state of their accommodation. He had expected nothing much more than a dingy dormitory. A single damp log cabin which they needed to share with a dozen other tourists. As was always the case with their holidays, it was Evelyn who had arranged everything. She had been the driving force for wanting to come here, to the Amazon. Patric supposed that if it had been up to him then he might never leave the city at all. Their cabin, though, in actual fact, was spacious, with twin beds, and an en suite bathroom. True, the water pressure was below the standard he felt comfortable with, and there was a lack of hot water.

As he circled the camp, coming to the point where the log walkway began, he almost collided with a fellow tourist. That was the problem with everything being in near darkness.

The other tourist clicked on a torch. He had a deep voice which squeaked in odd places. "Woah! Steady there! Where have you been?"

Patric took a few seconds to analyse the man's appearance. He had shoulder-length hair and wore a bandana wrapped about his forehead. He also wore glasses and had on a long dressing gown. "I was down by the water," Patric replied.

"Alone? Without a flashlight?"

Patric didn't much like the man's tone. "Yes. It got darker faster than I thought. Why?"

"Don't you remember the safety talk? That we're not to leave the camp without a guide when it gets dark? And never, under any circumstances, to go anywhere without a light?"

"I ... guess I forgot that part. Or I didn't think I was going to be that long. I thought I was going to get back before the sun set."

"Jesus. What a self-centred asshole."

"I'm sorry?"

"If one of us gets lost then they have to send out a search party. That's dangerous for everybody. Especially at night."

"Oh, I imagine they know these woods like the back of their hand. It's no skin off their nose. Isn't that why we pay to have guides? I mean, beyond them showing us around, they're here to keep us safe — "

"But only if we follow their rules, man."

Patric drew a deep breath. He never liked to lose control. Especially around strangers. There was no telling exactly who a stranger was, or who they might be connected to. But in this case, he decided to make an exception. "Hippies these days are different from what I remember — I never thought they'd be such sticklers for red tape.

"Hey, there's no need for name-calling, man. I'm just calling you out on your antisocial behaviour. What goes on in Yuppie Land is just fine. But we're in the jungle now. This is a different environment. We have to work together — be part of a greater whole. You're not the king. Not out here, anyway."

Patric knew he had riled the man. He always enjoyed these moments in conversations. He liked to give the impression he was the one losing control. He was a good actor. He had found that if he made his eyes bulge *just so* and if he snorted in *just such a way* he could make it seem that he was riled. "That's funny, my money still seems to work fine here."

The man narrowed his eyes. "You know, one day your money's not gonna work for you. And that day you'll learn a lesson." Shaking his head, he stalked away.

Patric allowed himself a slight smile.

Maybe he was self-centred.

Maybe he was vain.

But wasn't that the price of success?

———

Later that evening they had arranged a midnight canoe trip. After dinner, about half an hour to midnight, Patric waited patiently for

Evelyn to finish up in the bathroom, putting on her makeup. He wondered why she bothered. Was she worried about what the guides thought? Or whether the jaguars and caimans might whisper? Dinner had been piranha soup. It had been too spicy for his tastes and he wanted to brush his teeth to get shot of the flavour. As Evelyn left the bathroom, she caught his eye. "Oh, Jesus," she said.

"What?" Patric replied. "What's the problem? I didn't say anything."

"You don't *need* to say anything. I can read the expression on your face. I can tell just what you're thinking."

"And what am I thinking?"

"You're wondering why I'm taking so long to get ready — and you're now going to go in there and spend just as long doing lord-knows-what. On your Link, no doubt. Pressing virtual palms. Making online deals. *Improving* people's lives."

"Well, you don't need to worry about that out here. There's no connection. I tried down by the water and got chewed out by some hippy for angering the guides."

Evelyn shook her head. "You just know how to make friends, don't you? I honestly don't understand how you can get on day to day when you turn everyone into an enemy."

"The trick," Patric said, as he shimmied past her and into the waiting, empty bathroom, "is to know which people you can safely anger." As he readied to shut the door on her, he dropped his voice to a whisper. "Which people matter — and which people don't."

———

Despite Patric's constant self-reassurance that he was glad to embrace conflict, he was secretly pleased to find that the guide who would be leading their canoe trip that evening was not the same one from the jungle canopy expedition earlier in the day. Patric knew that he didn't actively go out seeking fights — he just had a difficult time keeping his mouth shut when he was confronted with something he didn't agree with. It was his firm belief that he was a reasonable person. Just that he didn't tolerate bullshit of any sort.

In the light from their head torches, he saw that their guide for the evening was a man in his seventies. Like them, he also wore a head torch. He had leathered skin, a puff of white hair beneath his baseball cap and black eyes peeping out of his wrinkled expression. He wore a bush shirt, a pair of khaki shorts, flip-flops. His body was that of a man in his forties. Patric supposed that was the result of a lifetime of physical labour.

A life of "useful" work as his father might've said.

The guide gave them a gurning grin, blinding them with his head torch as he did so. The canoe itself bobbed about at the side of the jetty while the guide held it still, waiting for Patric and Evelyn to clamber aboard. The canoe was just big enough for four at a squeeze, with two planks lying across the interior. In his torchlight, Patric noted the puddle of water sitting in the centre. "Looks like it's leaking."

The guide turned to Patric, blinding him again with his head torch. He grinned at him, clearly not comprehending what he had said.

Patric glanced at Evelyn, and she rolled her eyes. He decided he was best off leaving this particular battle. He stepped over the side and — taking a second while he stabilised himself in the centre of the canoe — took his place on one of the planks. Evelyn clambered in beside him. The guide jammed his fingers into his mouth and gave a hearty whistle. He received a response from the bank and then pushed them away from the jetty.

As they bobbed out onto the open water, the guide paddling

them gently along the bank, Patric felt the gentle warm breeze blowing over the river. The air was damp — as it always was here. He could hear the chatters out in the undergrowth of the jungle surrounding him. Up above, the clouds drifted by, giving glimpses of the inky purple night sky, the moon shining and the stars sparkling.

It was just as they were rounding the corner — leaving the lodges behind — that Patric felt the all-too-familiar vibrating sensation at his temple.

And then again.

And again.

New messages.

Acting on impulse, Patric flicked his retinal display on, seeing that his Link had managed to find a connection way out here. He examined his inbox. Seeing the messages flowing down the screen. People desperately wanting to get in touch with him. People who wanted his own personal brand of motivation to help them achieve their life goals. He recalled a time a few years ago when he had offered an emergency service called 911 Self Confidence. The idea had been to charge a premium so that those who wanted his advice could get in touch with him at any time of day or night. He thought about how Evelyn had viewed that particular proposal. She had thought that he was crazy ... actually, worse than that, after the first week, she had threatened to leave him if he continued. At home, they would be in the middle of dinner or taking an evening walk when someone would contact Patric in a panic ... and Patric would talk them down — talk some sense into them.

Patric was certain he could've made it work if Evelyn hadn't made such a scene. People were quick to point to the negatives involved with constant connection to the web but it was really more complex than that.

Nothing could be simplified so easily.

With all this in mind, Patric was careful to go undetected as he scanned through these messages, slipping Evelyn a glance every couple of seconds. But she was focused on the river bank, as was the guide, the two of them tracking the foliage for any sign of stirring wildlife. Patric had to admit that he didn't hold out all that much hope of seeing exotic animals on this trip. He had already spoken to several others before coming out here and he was realistic — the Amazon wasn't a zoo, after all.

As Patric read through one of his messages — from a now-quite-senior executive for a city bank — he wondered if he could get away with a reply. There was no telling when his signal might drop out. The executive was having trouble firing underperforming employees, what must have sat within the top five issues people in management positions came to him with regards to their working life. There was the guilt, of course. That was a complicated, sometimes nasty thing to reconcile. But it was beatable.

With the right coaching, of course.

"Unbelievable," Evelyn said.

Patric snapped back to reality. Away from his Link. He thought Evelyn would be staring right at him — admonishingly. However, she was still eyeing the river bank. Looking out for wildlife. He wondered if that was just another aspect of being vain or self-absorbed ... he believed the world revolved around him.

But, then again, didn't everyone think that?

Patric followed Evelyn's gaze to the river bank. The guide had stopped paddling. He could see — in the bright white light — a pair of slimy eyes looking out at them.

"Caiman," the guide said, in a reverential tone.

Patric looked at the thing through the gloom. The way the alligator's eyes sat on its head was unnerving. The eyes had the size and appearance of rotten pickled eggs. It was never obvious exactly where it was looking. It might be looking directly at him.

Or it might be glaring over his shoulder. To be quite honest he had never been the greatest fan of reptiles … although he had certainly been called one more than a handful of times in his life.

The guide stood up, making the canoe rock violently from side to side. Patric felt a quiver in his gut as he worried that he might tumble into the river.

But the canoe stabilised.

The guide slipped both his flip-flops off and dropped them into the centre of the boat. He then gestured at Patric and Evelyn, communicating that they should keep their head torches fixed on the caiman. He then slipped into the water.

The river wasn't as deep as Patric had thought — the water came just above the guide's waist. The guide crept closer, stalking the caiman.

Patric flipped a glance in Evelyn's direction, as if she would be equally concerned about what was transpiring, but she remained fixed on the sight before them.

The guide stood very still.

The caiman made no movement either.

Patric felt the breeze creeping along the river again. His heart beat slow and low, a steady pulse at his temples. It was hard to describe, but there was something which was just so animal about the scene. Predator and prey.

Life and death.

For the first time since he had arrived in the Amazon, Patric felt as if he had found that long-sought connection with nature. That he was seeing its raw power.

And then the guide struck.

It was over in less than two, three seconds, but Patric felt the terror of each of them passing by. He reached for Evelyn's hand, gripped it tightly. In the light from their head torches, he observed the guide grabbing the caiman from behind. After a brief struggle, with the thrashing of water, the guide emerged triumphant with the caiman draped over his arm, his hand carefully gripping its neck to prevent any sudden movements.

Patric gazed on the animal with wonder — and he noted Evelyn was doing the same.

The guide slowly made his way back to the canoe, turning side on. He looked to them both and then gestured with his hand for them to stroke the animal along the ridge of its back.

Patric felt immediately uneasy. He glanced at Evelyn seeing that she too was reluctant. Then he thought about why they had come to the Amazon in the first place. They were supposed to be having some sort of an "experience".

They were *supposed* to be experiencing the wildness of nature.

And handling this caiman was hardly that difficult.

The guide had secured it and he was clearly an expert handler. He was grinning from ear to ear as if he was a mere angler who had plucked a good-sized trout out of the water.

Patric sat up in the boat. Now that there was a caiman a matter of inches from his nose he found that he wasn't so bothered by the boat's movements beneath him.

He felt a thrill as he draped his fingers along the caiman's jagged back. It was like stroking a piece of smoothed-over volcanic rock. Then again, he supposed that these creatures were from the time when volcanoes were commonplace across the globe. As he traced his fingers up the creature's spine, his focus shifted back to those eyes. He saw how they continued to stare at him. He felt himself becoming caught in the slitted pupils, like a pair of crevices in a piece of rock.

It was now that the wind picked up significantly.

A harsh gust blew across the water.

And everything happened quickly.

The guide stumbled, staggered, and then lost his footing.

He fell into the water with a splash.

Patric tried to yank his hand away.

But it was too late.

There was a flash.

Pain.

A kind of numbed shock at first. And then it retreated. Patric's logical thoughts returned. He looked down at his arm — the source of pain.

All he saw was blood.

His blood.

He folded over himself, gripping his injured arm to his belly, as if he might be expecting another attack. He gazed wildly about, into the water with his head torch. He saw a stirring in the water several yards away. The caiman had escaped.

The guide stood back up in the water. He had been completely submerged when he had fallen. His eyes widened and his mouth gaped when he saw Patric's injury. He made gasping sounds, as if the sight was beyond all reason.

As Patric felt the warm blood dribble out of him, everything was becoming woozier. As he began to feel fainter and fainter, he thought about how if he had been back in the city his Link would've been contacting the emergency services right about now. That it would be feeding back real-time vital information to the team of expert emergency operators so when they arrived on the scene they were prepared to offer fully customised care.

Now, though, he was in the middle of the jungle.

There weren't any emergency services here.

Nothing to rely on.

Patric was half conscious of the trip back to the lodges. Evelyn was beside him, urging him to compress the wound with his shirt. She kept on asking him basic questions, as if she was more afraid that he was losing his mind than that he was about to black out. At some point in the encounter with the caiman, his head torch had come loose and been lost. And so now he had only the dim illumination provided by the moon — its light just about penetrating the thick cloud which'd gathered overhead.

As they approached the jetty, the guide whistled high and piercingly. Patric supposed that this meant there was an emergency because several other guides rushed to meet them.

Among their number, Patric couldn't help but notice the guide who had led them on the canopy excursion earlier in the day.

Three or four guides helped Patric from the canoe — a feat which was not made simple due to the nature of his injury. He was then briskly hurried off to the central lodge, where they were provided with their meals.

In the bright light of the main lodge, Patric saw that there were two or three other tourists sat slumped in chairs, looking out over the river. All of them sat upright, turning in their seats to take in the sight of Patric arriving.

Patric couldn't help but notice the hippy from earlier among them. Even through his pain, he felt a slight itch of discomfort in his stomach at seeing him here … in this condition. The hippy no doubt thought that he had been proven right. That some act of Patric's foolishness had led him to this predicament.

Speaking rapid-fire Portuguese around him, the guides eased Patric down onto a seat at one of the tables. One of them gripped Patric's elbow, placing his arm around in front of him and onto the table. Patric was reluctant to remove the compress of his shirt on the wound but he didn't have the strength to resist. There was a muttered command and from somewhere a wad of white bedlinen was produced. This was laid across the table, beneath Patric's injured arm. It was only now that Patric was able to study his injury in any kind of detail.

The caiman had got hold of the flesh just above his wrist — and he could see where it had torn. Blood dripped down onto the bedsheet. The coppery scent caught in his nostrils, making him a little giddy. He glanced up, catching Evelyn's eye from where she stood nearby. Seeing her surprise frightened him.

"That's gonna need stitches."

Patric recognised the voice. Sure enough, he turned to see the long hair held in place by the bandana, the glasses. The hippy.

Patric felt the pulse of pain at the wound site. Although his common sense hadn't quite deserted him, it wasn't quite with him, either. He couldn't help but say, "Sorry?"

"Give me a second, I'll go get my stuff."

Even despite the situation, Patric couldn't help but feel the chafe of the confrontation they had had earlier that evening. When he spoke, his tone was more than a little bitter. "What stuff?"

But the hippy had already gone.

Patric thought about how — if he had been back in the city — he would've been in the expert care of some MedDroid. There was just no infrastructure for them out here. No connection to any CPU — no major power source where they could recharge. For all of their progress in the last century, the majority of human innovations were still most at home in urban environments. Cities.

The hippy returned with a bag about the size of a woman's large handbag. He sat at the table beside Patric while the guides watched on. He snapped the bag open and laid out supplies.

"You're a doctor?" Patric asked, but this time when he spoke, he was disappointed by the bitterness in his voice. He hadn't intended it. He saw now that this hippy ... this *man* ... was only trying to help him.

"Nurse."

Patric watched him lay out sutures, cotton wool, iodine.

"This is my emergency kit," the hippy said. "I can't really carry anything more than this and be practical." Apparently happy with what he had produced from his medical kit, the hippy sat back, sighed and then looked at Patric. "Unfortunately I don't have any anaesthetic — I haven't been able to get hold of it here and it's the sort of thing that gets you into trouble at borders."

Patric absorbed this statement a moment, realising what it meant. When he spoke this time, his voice was thin, reedy. "Will it hurt?"

The hippy met his eye. "Quite a bit — yeah."

————

Patric should have known that when a medical professional told him that something was going to hurt it was going to be bad. At first, he convinced himself he would ease into the pain — that it would gradually get better as time went on. But that proved not to be the case. Each time the hippy pierced his skin, he felt that hot, searing pain afresh.

He supposed the whole procedure took no more than half an hour but it felt like a marathon eight- or nine-hour operation. When it was over, Patric still felt the pain above his wrist, but added to this was the pinching sensation of where the man had set the sutures. The hippy gave him some pills to take for the pain and they made Patric feel slightly woozy.

Sitting back, checking his work with a self-critical eye, the hippy seemed satisfied and glanced at Patric. "My name's Lewis, by the way. I don't think we ever introduced ourselves to one another, did we?"

"Patric," he replied, extending his good hand for Lewis to shake. "Thank you," Patric managed to get out. "And I'm ... sorry ... you know, for earlier. For being stubborn. You're right. It wasn't responsible. I should've taken more care." He turned to examine the guides standing around — picking out the guide from earlier that day and then the older guide who had taken them on the canoe trip. He couldn't help but notice the older guide looking sombre, an expression of guilt spread across his features. "And I'm sorry if I've been short, or inappropriate with anything I've said to any of you. You have to understand that I'm outside of my own habitat. This isn't a place where I feel comfortable — or where I am entitled to express my opinions." Even as the words tumbled out past his lips, Patric couldn't believe what he was saying.

Which wasn't the same as not being able to believe his words.

Finally, Patric turned to Evelyn, standing cautiously nearby. He knew that she probably thought he was reacting badly to the medication. That he was seconds away from throwing some sort of a fit. "And, Evie, I'm sorry too. For everything."

Strangely, Patric felt a slight dampness about the corners of his eyes. He hadn't cried since he had been a child and he was determined not to do so now. He swallowed back the tears, shifting his attention to his sutured arm. "Well, if nothing else, I have a story to tell. A scar to show off ... it's not every man who faces off with an alligator and lives to tell the tale."

HOPE IS A HORIZON

L anica peered through the porthole, out into space. Her forehead pressed against the cool glass, she spied the approaching shuttle. It was sending a distress signal — a gentle *ping-ping* alert sounded in her earpiece. The ship was requesting permission to dock.

Lanica felt tension spreading across her chest. All her muscles seized up tight. She breathed in the sharp, metallic scent of her ship, tasted it at the back of her mouth.

She had been here before. Her instincts told her to refuse the request. That she should fire the thrusters and get as far away from this place as possible.

But her conscience overrode her.

Gave her pause for thought.

Down there — down on Circius-8 — a battle was raging. Two groups of colonisers. A land-grab. The story was always the same. One family clan trying to drive out another — trying to drive the other out into space. It always made Lanica feel just a touch distressed for the future of humankind when a pair of families were unable to coexist on a planet a quarter of the size of Earth. Then again she supposed it was all just a question of human greed.

And there never seemed any limits to that.

She thought about the approaching shuttle some more. No doubt there was someone — or several people — who required urgent medical attention.

Wasn't that what she was here for?

The whole point of her assignment?

She had been sent here to patch people up. To put back together the fallen brothers, sisters, cousins, uncles and aunts. Wounded paramilitaries.

Wasn't this the reason why she had become a doctor — to help people?

If so then why was she running away?

Or perhaps it was more complicated than that. Maybe there were some she had decided were more worthy of her help than others.

She thought about the laser cannon. About how she could call out a few commands and have it target the approaching shuttle.

Remove it from existence.

Then what?

A harsher, repetitive tone in Lanica's earpiece told her that the shuttle was attempting to open comms. She wondered if they had noted her hesitancy. Logic returned to her and she opened the channel to communicate. "Horizon F4 – On humanitarian assignment," Lanica said, on autopilot. "Please state the nature of your emergency."

Their end of the line was filled with static. She could only make out every other word. "Hello? ... got ... bleeding ... gone ... evacuate ..."

The adrenaline kicked in as it always did. Lanica's heart pounded away at her temples. But she managed to keep herself calm, measured. It was strange how her reaction to pressure had always been like this. Somehow she always managed to detach herself from the situation. To see it with cool neutrality.

"I'm having trouble making out your message. Please confirm origin and souls on board." She thought for another second, seeing that her ship systems had identified the shuttle. It belonged to the O'Neill family clan. She saw that it was registered unarmed, although there was little chance of that being true. The only thing she could say for certain was that her ship would be able to outrun it given a clear chance ... even if the O'Neills had fit it with some kind of overamped, concealed thrusters.

This time when she opened comms with the shuttle, there was no response at all.

Only static.

Her thoughts kicked on harder than ever. She wondered if there had been some failure in the life-support systems. If those on-board were choking to death through lack of oxygen, or else being boiled alive due to a failure in the cooling technology.

That was enough.

She couldn't take it any longer.

She accepted the request to dock.

———

Lanica stepped into her overalls — a full-body garment which encompassed sturdy boots and low-level protection for exposure to radiation. There was also the mental aspect. Lanica couldn't deny that once she had zipped up her overalls, when she held her medi-pack down at her thigh, she felt as though she was ready for anything.

On her way up to the dock, she strapped on her blaster.

It seemed to satisfy the feeling telling her to be cautious.

Her Link fed her retinal display, shifting through a checklist which she needed to manually complete. It was checking up on her equipment — testing her readiness. When it told her she had achieved one-hundred-percent, she tried to feel positive.

In truth, she knew it was impossible to be ready for anything.

Standing at the dock, Lanica observed the pitch and roll as the shuttle went through its landing pattern. It was shaped like one of those garbage cans she would observe people using to burn leaves in the old films she would watch. It had been kicked and bent out of shape in the same way, too. As the shuttle got closer, she saw the laser-cannon burns. Some of them looked fresh — especially the large gash in the hull.

The outer hatch of her ship swooped back to allow the shuttle through. The shuttle came to rest upon the landing plat-form. Its landing gear were damaged so it rolled slightly to one side before coming to rest as the localised gravitational field came into play. In what seemed like no time at all, the inner airlock was opening and the landing platform was moving toward her.

She gripped the medipack more tightly. And she couldn't help but feel reassured by the steady weight of her blaster pistol at the small of her back.

The shuttle door slid open.

A wild-eyed man, with bright-blue eyes, and shoulder-length sandy hair, burst from within. His face was smeared with dried blood. His helmet dangled down from his life-support pack. Apparently he had discarded it swiftly on landing. "Quick — please!"

Lanica held her ground a moment, and then her medical instincts took over. She followed the man in through the open shuttle door.

Even as she stepped into the shuttle, she smelled the blood. It crept up her nostrils and down the back of her throat. She felt every hair in her body stand on end. Her heart threatened to burst her eardrums. And yet the calm descended — as it always did.

She pictured herself as some small, easily frightened mammal ... a squirrel ... a field mouse ... the trick was to recognise the animal instinct and move beyond it.

That was what made her human.

The shuttle was not large. It barely had enough space to accommodate the four colonisers within and herself. A cursory glance at the ship cockpit revealed a glittering sea of red lights. A synthesised voice was chirping "warning, warning," over and over again.

She turned her attention to the patients before her.

They were slumped up against the side of the shuttle.

All but one of them had removed their helmets.

With a stirring motion in her gut, Lanica decided that this coloniser was dead. She didn't need to scan the person with her Link to know the truth. She could see the blood soaking their overalls. The unmistakable ragdoll quality of a body bereft of life.

To mitigate the shock, she tried to lie to herself — to tell herself there was something inhuman about the coloniser. She couldn't discern the gender. No face. Nothing more than a ragdoll ... and she could keep telling herself that lie until later when she would need to register the death. Then the truth would hit home.

Lanica looked to the other three, the man who she had first seen, and then the other two lying on the ground. Two women.

Lanica got down on her knees, springing open her medipack with a single practised gesture. She glanced over the two women, instantly noticing the bleeding at the neck and abdomen of the first; the way the second woman's leg stuck out at an odd angle. Somehow she was able to push their scrunched-up faces, the constant moans and groans of pain, to one side of her consciousness. She supposed something within her brain told her they wouldn't help her to do a better job.

With her Link reading off diagnostics into the earpiece — heart rate, estimated blood oxygen levels, body temperature — she did her best to think clearly. She pulled out a patching spray, stopping the flow of blood at the first woman's neck. The woman said nothing as she worked. She could tell that she was barely still with her. Back inside her medipack, Lanica pulled out a box knife. She worked at the material on the woman's fatigues, sawing away. The blade of the knife snapped.

"Here," the woman with the broken leg replied. "Take mine."

Lanica eyed the knife held out to her. It was an enormous thing — a bush-hunting knife. And it was covered with dried blood. In theory, she should go back and get a sanitised one from her own supplies. But that would waste precious time.

She took the knife and carefully continued to work at the woman's fatigues. When she sighted the wound, she did her best to suppress a gasp. It was gaping. If Lanica had to guess, she would've said the woman had taken a laser blast direct to the belly.

She eyed the woman's face, seeing that her eyes were pressed shut, that she was on the brink of losing consciousness. If she didn't act fast there would be two corpses in this shuttle before long. Lanica used most of the rest of the spray can to patch up the damage.

As she moved onto the woman with the broken leg, she was all too aware that the wound in the other woman's abdomen was still weeping. The woman would need to undergo surgery as soon as possible. But first Lanica needed to triage the woman with the broken leg to make sure she wasn't missing anything equally urgent.

Lanica did her best to concentrate — not thinking about the woman's abdomen — while she reviewed the woman with the broken leg.

The Link read back the vital signs.

Everything was stable — slightly elevated as she would expect from someone undergoing an injury such as this but otherwise fine. She administered an anaesthetic and then spoke over her shoulder to the man standing over them. "Help her up. Take her to the medbay. Check your Link if you get lost. If the Link can't make a local connection follow the signs." She sensed the man dawdling — no more than a few seconds, but seconds were precious in these sorts of situations. "Get a move on!"

Her command had the desired effect. The man crouched down and — with the woman crying out in pain — he helped her onto her good foot.

Lanica watched them disappear from sight. Somehow she felt calmer now. Perhaps it was because she no longer felt like she was being watched. Even after all of these years of experience, she supposed she had never quite got used to the whole performance aspect of her job — of having people standing around *watching*.

As it was on her mind, she returned her attention to the woman's abdomen. Just as she had expected, it was still weeping. She considered this for a moment. And then she issued an order for a MedDroid. She needed to get the woman into surgery right away.

Within a minute, the MedDroid arrived. It was MedDroid B — a pastel-blue colour. It ran on wheels, not coming any higher than her knee. It pushed along a crash trolley, as she had instructed. She would have called up a MedDroid for the woman with the broken leg, only that MedDroid A was undergoing repairs. And there was no question in her mind about which of the women's needs were greater at this moment in time.

With its hydraulic arms, its gentle, unfurling fingers, the MedDroid helped her lift the woman onto the crash trolley. "Okay, take her away."

Unlike the man, the droid didn't hesitate. That was the wonderful thing about machines. They took orders without question.

Soon enough, she was alone with the body.

Everything seemed suddenly so still.

So silent.

It was only now that she took stock of how her heart throbbed within her ribcage. Her face must be bright red. She pressed her hands to her hips and eyed the motionless colonist.

And then there was some activity on her Link.

A heartbeat — *faint* — but a heartbeat all the same.

The colonist wasn't dead.

————

"Hello? Can you hear me?"

Lanica was down on her knees at the side of the colonist. That would teach her to take the appearance of a situation for granted. She hadn't thought to check the vitals. All her attention had been for the two women. She had supposed that the reason they hadn't removed this colonist's helmet was because they knew the person was dead … and that the helmet was now some kind of death mask — never to be removed.

She reached out for the helmet, searching for the release clasp. She found it. Working gently, keeping one eye on the weakening heartbeat in the corner of her retinal display, she lifted the helmet off and laid it to one side.

Another man.

This one had coal-black skin and chalky white hair. There was almost no motion on his face — no obvious evidence to back up his vital signs.

But she knew the heartbeat was still there.

She rifled through her medipack, hoping to find something.

Her mind had gone blank.

How had she missed this?

Was she losing her edge?

Was it time for her to go home?

What even was "home" now?

"Don't … don't …"

Lanica swivelled on the spot. Her heart rattled against her

eardrums. She tried to keep herself still. Attempted to keep herself calm on some level.

But it was easier said than done.

She stared at the man, seeing his lips had turned a shade of blue.

His eyelids were slightly open. She could just make out the watery surface of his eyeballs. "Don't *trust* ... don't ..." He took a shuddering breath and then his whole body seemed to sigh.

Lanica knew exactly what that meant. And she switched into her routine without even thinking about it. She maneuvered the man onto his back and went about performing CPR. Her whole body was shaking as she noted how cold his skin was. How it seemed as if he had already died several minutes ago. But she had definitely seen him looking at her. She had heard the words he had spoken.

Don't trust.

———

There was no time for Lanica to think about the dead man. She supposed that was what made her profession bearable. Traumas were all around her, but there was always something urgent that she should be doing. Something to distract her attention.

She was in surgery for over four hours. It was a mess. And it took the greater part of her medical training to even begin on it. Every time she felt that she was turning a corner, she was knocked back. A fresh bleed. Something she had missed. But somehow she got through.

Her faithful MedDroid B helped her during surgery, providing her with an extra set of hands. Although it would not be able to comprehend what she meant by it if she had said so much out loud, the droid also provided her with some much-needed companionship.

When Lanica finished — somehow patching up the patient and returning her to a stable condition — she was totally exhausted. Usually, she felt a sense of achievement after such a long case but not today.

She instructed MedDroid B to execute the recovery process, and she watched on with the detachment of an observer as the droid moved the patient out of the operating theatre and into the recovery room. Next the droid would do a deep clean on the theatre — to ready it for the next patient ... whoever that might be.

Lanica had almost forgotten about the man with the sandy hair and the woman with the broken leg. She eyed them both outside the operating theatre. There were a pair of sofas and the woman was lying down on one of them while the man was splayed over the other.

The man sat himself upright when he saw her. "How is she?"

"In recovery," Lanica replied stifling a yawn.

"Can we see her?"

"She'll take a little while to come around."

"But can we see her?"

There was a tone of insistence in the man's voice. It suggested that she was challenging him when she had merely been stating the facts. She waved in the direction of the partially frosted glass which looked into the recovery room.

He went over to look.

Meanwhile, Lanica eyed the woman with the broken leg. She saw that her eyes were partially open. That she was awake. "We'll get some plaster on that once the MedDroid is finished."

The woman remained straight-faced, as if she hadn't heard Lanica. "Thanks," she said, her words distant.

Lanica looked to the man, still standing at the glass, checking up on the woman's recovery. "Is she going to be okay?" he asked.

"It's too early. We need to wait."

"But what do you reckon — will she make it?"

"I hope so."

The man pouted at her then shifted his attention onto the woman with the broken leg. Finally, he turned back to Lanica. "You're up here all alone."

For a split second Lanica was tempted to lie. But, in the end, she knew such a lie would prove impossible to keep up. They would find out eventually. "All except my droids."

The man scoffed. "Person goes crazy in the company of just droids."

"Is that so?"

"I would."

"Do you think I'm crazy?"

The man half closed one eye, sizing her up. "I ... dunno yet."

Lanica felt another yawn coming on. She really needed to rest. The patient was stable for the time being but an alarm might go off in her earpiece at any moment, summoning her back into the theatre to continue her patch job.

She looked beyond the man, into the recovery room. She saw that the droid had docked itself in the recharge bay. She wondered if she should let it recover for a little bit.

"So what happened to the rest of your crew?" the man asked. "You didn't go postal and drop them out the airlock?"

Although the man was trying to lighten the atmosphere, she really wasn't in the mood. And wasn't there something slightly sinister about his tone — something she couldn't quite put her finger on? Maybe it was what the other colonist had said right before he had died.

Perhaps that had put her on edge.

Don't trust.

Lanica forced a smile, doing her best to show the man that she had taken his joke in good humour. "I'll show you to some cabins where you can get rested up."

"What about my leg?" the woman asked, her voice sleepy, apparently still affected by the anaesthesia.

Lanica thought about the scans. She needed to get it immobilised but she wanted to give the droid a chance to recharge after such a long stint in the operating theatre. "I'll give you some crutches now and plaster it first thing in the morning." She paused, wondering if she should stop talking now, but there was something about fatigue which loosened her tongue. "I ... don't want to make a mistake."

Neither the man or the woman said anything to this, but she felt the tension enter the air as it always did whenever a doctor admitted that they were human after all.

———

Lanica woke several times during the night. She was certain her earpiece was rousing her. Calling her back to the theatre. Each time, however, there was nothing.

Only stillness.

The ship's cooling system.

The distant hum of the engines.

All the sounds she was accustomed to.

Before she had gone to bed, she had instructed MedDroid B to transport the dead man to the morgue, where an autopsy would be performed by the ship's systems. There was little doubt in her mind as to the cause of death. It was the nature of autopsies that they could usually do little to determine the circumstances surrounding the death — and that was what most interested her. If

MedDroid B had found anything worthy of human investigation, it would have summoned her from her slumber. She would revise the report the next day.

When the gradual glow of the ship's lighting signalled morning, Lanica unwound herself from her bedsheets. Her whole body ached. She knew one of her greatest weaknesses during surgery was how her shoulders would go rigid. How tension would tighten across her upper back. And the worst part was that she wouldn't notice how tense she was getting until the next day. When her muscles ached horribly.

She saw that the man and the woman had made it to the ship's canteen. Although she knew on a logical level that this was only to be expected — the ship would have guided the two of them through their Links to the canteen so that they might get breakfast — she also felt a sense of invasion to see these two people here, on *her* ship.

Well, it wasn't *her* ship.

She was on assignment.

Here to do a job.

And this ship was her workplace ...

After a while, though — especially alone — it seemed much more than that.

The canteen was cosy, or Lanica thought so when she was in there alone. Today, it felt cramped with the man tucking into a bowl of cereal, the woman with her hands on some canned peaches and a couple of slices of toast. Both had a cup of coffee steaming away on the table before them. They wore clean white-grey robes, again provided to them by the ship. And again this seemed almost like some kind of betrayal.

"Morning," the man said. "I tried to get in to see her but the ship wouldn't let me."

"The medbay is secured," Lanica replied.

For a second, Lanica thought the man might challenge this. If he might make some scene about them being "treated like criminals". But in the end he just bowed his head and continued to munch on his cereal.

"We'll get you in plaster after breakfast," Lanica said, speaking to the woman.

She gave her a slight smile. "Thanks."

Lanica should've put the plaster on last night. It wouldn't have taken her and the MedDroid more than five, ten minutes. What had she meant when she had said that she was afraid of making a mistake? Plastering fractures was straightforward. And even if she had made a mistake it wouldn't have been difficult to fix ... that had been a mistake, and it was better not to make mistakes around strangers.

Especially when you were unsure whether or not you could trust them.

"How is she this morning?" the man asked.

Lanica thought back to the read-out she had seen on the Link. "Stable. But she needs to rest."

"Not through the woods, huh?"

"You could say that."

"You gonna get some breakfast for yourself?"

More than anything, Lanica wanted to get out of the canteen, put some distance between herself and these two. She knew she could come up with some excuse, the most obvious would be to say that she had to check on the woman's recovery. But that might make her look less confident, less sure of herself.

And this was *her* ship ... she didn't care about the details.

"Yeah," she replied, flipping open a cupboard and selecting a pot of instant noodles. She applied boiling water, grabbed a fork, and then sat at the table with the man and the woman.

"I'm Pete — this here's Cheshire. *Chessy.*" The man jerked his thumb in the direction of the medbay. "That there's Ronelle. *Ron*, or *Ronny* if you're familiar."

Lanica stabbed at her noodles. "And who was the other man, down in the shuttle?"

"Magic."

" 'Magic' ?"

The man — Pete — finished off his cereal, dropping his spoon inside with a clatter. "That was what he called himself." He swilled the dregs of coffee about the bottom of the cup and then tossed what remained down his throat. "Wasn't nothing to be done for him, was there?"

Lanica shook her head.

A silence pressed down upon them.

"And your name is ...?" Pete asked.

"Lanica."

"Lanny?"

"No."

"Icky?" the woman — Chessy — put in.

Lanica sniffed a laugh. "No."

"Then what'd we call you?" Pete asked.

"Lanica. Or Doctor Smith."

"See, Chessy, didn't I always tell you how medics are up themselves? Must be all that time they spend alone studying. All that *knowledge* they got in their heads. Makes them better than the rest of us."

"Pete," Chessy replied, in a chiding tone. "She did just save Ronny's life."

Pete tilted his head to one side, apparently seeing the error of his ways. He caught Lanica's eye for a moment but she didn't want to hold his gaze for longer than that. "Sorry, doc, I didn't mean nothing by it. That's just the way I am, okay?"

"Okay," Lanica replied. When she judged that long enough

had gone by to make it seem as though all was forgotten and she wasn't simply trying to change the subject, Lanica addressed Chessy. "Shall we take a look at getting your leg in plaster?"

———

While Lanica worked with MedDroid B on plastering Chessy's leg, she couldn't help but find her mind drifting onto her other patient, Ronelle. She wanted to take another look at her as soon as possible. She knew that vital signs could be deceiving in the same way that earthquake alarms only went off after the initial tremor.

Once Lanica was through, she ushered Chessy out on her crutches, getting rid of Pete at the same time, telling him he needed to keep her company because of the sedative she had been administered. Lanica slipped into the recovery room.

She looked back through the information issuing through her Link, and then flipped it all off and gazed down on her patient.

Ronelle lay still, lying on her back on the bed. Her face gave nothing away. If Lanica hadn't known better she might've thought that Ronelle was having a pleasant dream. But Lanica knew that it was touch and go. That laser blast had burned straight through her gut. She had done her best to patch things up but she knew the reality of any gut injury from a laser blast ... the prognosis was never good.

It happened quickly.

Ronelle suddenly came around, her eyelids flipping open and her mouth gasping for air. A jolt passed up Lanica's spine. Her heart beat wildly. But she calmed herself almost instantly, as she had trained herself over many years of dealing with trauma cases. After all this "experience" she couldn't help but wonder whether she wasn't the traumatised one.

Ronelle glared about the recovery room. "Are they ... are they here?"

It took Lanica a second to process just who Ronelle meant by "they". "No," Lanica replied. "They're in another part of the ship."

"You rescued them too?"

"Yes, you were on the same shuttle."

Ronelle screwed up her eyes. Her complexion went pallid. When she responded, her voice was a croak. "Why, oh *why!*"

Lanica was all too aware of the read-outs on her Link. Everything was pointing to another anaesthetic being administered. But at the same time she knew that would make Ronelle woozy — she might drop off. And she wanted to hear what she had to say.

Lanica leaned in closer. Dropped her voice to a whisper. "What happened down there?"

Ronelle stared into her eyes. Although Lanica had never had any belief about spiritualism or the like — unless *disbelief* qualified — she could've sworn that Ronelle was peering into her mind. Then her focus shifted. She looked down at Lanica's wrist. "I ... I have the same tattoo."

To begin with Lanica was taken off-guard by the change in Ronelle's tone of voice. How it had taken on a dreamlike quality. As if she had administered her with an anaesthetic.

Lanica looked at her own wrist as if she had forgotten.

"Hope is a horizon," Ronelle said.

Lanica eyed the words on the inside of her wrist. The words written beneath the heel of her palm in a square script. She looked to Ronelle again. "Where's your tattoo?"

Ronelle squeezed her eyes shut and then swallowed hard.

A quick glance at the read-outs showed Lanica's heartrate climbing dangerously. She really needed to act ... and not soon ... she needed to act *now*.

Ronelle found the strength to return. Her eyes were streaming with tears now. Her whole body trembling. She tilted her head slightly, indicating her shoulders. As she fixed her eyes on her, Lanica realised she was waiting for her to take a look.

"I need to give you something," Lanica said. "I'll take a look in a moment, okay?" Lanica half turned away, wanting to summon MedDroid B to her side so as to be as ready as she could be for any unanticipated complications.

Ronelle grabbed hold of her wrist, squeezing her with a strong grip which betrayed her condition. "Look now," she said. "I want you to see. Soon it will be too late."

" 'Too late' ? Why?"

"Please look."

Lanica remained where she was. She summoned up the option to administer the anaesthetic. She had no choice but to put Ronelle under. And yet she didn't ...

Ronelle used what must've been the last of her strength to lift herself up slightly from her pillow. Lanica looked at her back, unsure exactly what to expect. In the strong bright light of the recovery room, she eyed the tattoo, identical to her own but for one detail. The "is" had been crossed out and a crudely drawn "was" written beneath.

When Lanica carefully helped Ronelle back down onto the pillow, she saw that she was smiling, her whole face creasing with the expression. As if this was the funniest joke ever told. "Colonists never give up, do they?" Ronelle said, her voice as strong as it had been. "That's what it means. That's what it *meant*."

"I still believe it," Lanica replied. "We've got to. Everything has to be better in the future, otherwise what's the point? What if —"

A screeching tone tore through Lanica's eardrums. Her earpiece alerting her. She brought her retinal display back into the foreground of her vision. She saw the dire read-outs on Ronelle's condition and she did what she could to react quickly.

To use her training.

Her *knowledge*.

The knowledge that Pete had sneered at.

But it was too late.

———

In the ship's canteen, Pete drove his fist into one of the cabinet doors. "Argh!"

Lanica continued to stand where she was. "I'm sorry," she said. "I ... there was nothing I could do. She was badly injured."

Cheshire — *Chessy* — just sat at the table, head in hands, staring at her empty cup.

Lanica knew from experience that the best thing she could do right now was to step outside. To leave these people alone with their grief. Allow them to deal with it in a private manner. She hadn't had any connection to Ronelle, after all.

She had only failed to save her life.

However, although her logical mind told her to step out, her body refused to do its bidding. There was something about these two. Something which told her that she should put as much distance between herself and them as soon as she could.

"Where are you headed? I can set course. Make way. That's unless you're expecting more casualties? More shuttles?"

Neither one of them responded.

Lanica scolded herself for having spoken at all. She turned to leave now.

"Why do you do this, doctor?" Chessy said.

Lanica held her ground. She glanced back.

Chessy continued to stare into her cup. "Why're you up here

all on your own? Why're you drifting about, picking up the pieces of a battle you are neutral of?" She shifted her attention onto her. "You religious?"

"No," Lanica replied, and then deciding to qualify this, "not in any organised way."

"Then why?"

"I want to help people. I want to give something — "

"But look who you're helping! Bunch of rogues like us. What's our value? What do we add to the universe except thinning out our own numbers, huh? You save one of us, first thing we bullet right back into the melee, take up the fighting where it left off. You have no side. You'd save one of them equally as you'd save one of us. You're just pushing us closer to a stalemate each time. Making things go on longer. Making the pain last and — "

"Enough, Chrissy," Pete said, his voice measured, reasonable, as he cradled his bleeding knuckles. "We ain't got business asking questions. It's the doctor's own mind. Nobody else's." When he met Lanica's eye, she felt a quiver deep down in her gut. "Just as she ain't got no business asking us questions. That's our business. Ain't that right, doctor?"

Lanica thought of the dying man. How he had told her not to trust these two. And then she thought of Ronelle. Her reaction to the news that she had saved Chrissy and Pete too.

Weren't there enough red flags?

"That's right," Lanica replied.

"Good," Pete replied. "Then we've got an understanding." He sucked in breath through his nostrils, making a gravelly sound as he did so. "To answer your question, you can take us out past the system limits. Out to Belgravia-4. We can take care of things from there."

"You're not going back down? Back into the fray?"

Pete scoffed. "Doctor, I thought we had a deal? No questions."

Lanica flushed.

Pete peered down at his feet, as if he could see straight through the ship's fuselage. "That there's a lost cause if ever I saw one. And I never was much of a fighter for causes in the first place — unless that cause was for my own benefit."

A stillness sat on the canteen.

Lanica swallowed. "Okay — I'll set the coordinates."

———

Lanica stood at the port, watching MedDroid B load the two body cases onto the shuttle. When they got down onto Belgravia-4, the bodies would be duly processed and disposed of in accordance with their defunct users' wishes — whatever they might be.

Chessy and Pete stood alongside, observing the spectacle. There was something about being around other people that warmed her blood. Something about human contact. Soon she would be alone again, save for MedDroid B ... and MedDroid A once the repairs were concluded.

When the bodies had been loaded, the three of them eyed one another, as if unsure quite how to handle the farewell. She knew there was suspicion on all sides — and suspicion seldom led to ease of communication.

Right as Lanica was certain the two of them would stride onto the shuttle without uttering so much as another word to her, Chessy flung herself forward, her crutches clattering to the floor, grasping hold of Lanica around her neck. The motion was so sudden, so violent, that Lanica was certain she was trying to put her in a headlock. In those moments, Lanica cursed herself for having been so naïve. For not reading the hints.

For trusting these two.

But she soon realised that Chessy's hold was soft. That she was hugging her.

It was a long time since Lanica had been hugged.

And she was ashamed to admit that it was all over sooner than she would've liked.

When Chessy had peeled herself away from her, trod onto the shuttle with a muttered thank you, Lanica was still reeling. Soon, though, it was just her and Pete.

"Well, good luck," Pete said, holding out his hand.

Lanica pressed his palm, giving him a firm smile.

"You're brave, doc, I'll give you that much credit. I wouldn't be able to do what you do — not even if I had the brains. Just not wired that way, I guess."

Lanica nodded at this truism.

As Pete released her hand from his, he noticed the underside of her wrist. He smiled to himself and shook his head as he walked away, heading across the gangplank, and then disappearing into the shuttle belly.

Lanica stood by and watched on — MedDroid B at her side — as the shuttle shifted out through the airlock, drifting back out into space, headed on a planetside trajectory.

She watched the shuttle until she could no longer make it out against the darkness of space. Once it was gone, everything seemed so still. She felt almost as if she had just said goodbye to some old friends. That was the way she always felt, though.

Sentimentality only went so far but it had brought her here.

She glanced at the words written on her wrist another time — as she did multiple times a day — and then she smiled to herself and wandered back into her ship.

There were others out there.

Others to save.

AUTHOR'S NOTE

Thank you for taking the time to read one of my books. If you would like to hear about my latest releases you can sign up for my newsletter here: www.raymondsflex.com

Thanks for reading!

Raymond S Flex

Collected Science Fiction Short Stories
Volume Six

Copyright © Raymond S Flex, 2019.
Published by DIB Books, 2019.
All rights reserved.

Cover design and layout copyright © DIB Books, 2019.
Cover art copyright © Angela Harburn / Shutterstock, 2019.

www.ingramcontent.com/pod-product-compliance
Lightning Source LLC
Chambersburg PA
CBHW031218260626
47169CB00007B/2097